JUSTIFIED CONSPIRACY

Justified Conspiracy

Kelly Phillips

iUniverse, Inc.

New York Lincoln Shanghai

Justified Conspiracy

iUniverse books may be ordered through booksellers or by contacting:

iUniverse
2021 Pine Lake Road, Suite 100
Lincoln, NE 68512
www.iuniverse.com
1-800-Authors (1-800-288-4677)

ISBN-13: 978-0-595-37254-6 (pbk)
ISBN-13: 978-0-595-81651-4 (ebk)
ISBN-10: 0-595-37254-6 (pbk)
ISBN-10: 0-595-81651-7 (ebk)

Printed in the United States of America

In memory of the following wonderful people: Sean, my brother, Frieda and Nina, my grandmothers. I'm blessed to have shared in their energies of life and love.

Acknowledgements

This story unfolded through the development of the characters. Once created, these people did what they wanted, no matter what I told them to do. I captured what was happening, and that is how this novel was born. However, I had to find time to put the words onto the paper, and my sons had to be patient with me. Thanks, David and Michael, for understanding. Someone had to encourage me to publish the book. Thanks, dear husband, Mark, for being so supportive. People had to let me bounce ideas off of them. Thanks to my sisters, Diana and Billie-Jo, and my friend, Angie, for letting me do that. I had to stay in good health while writing. Thanks, Dad, for all your herbal remedies, and thanks, Aunt Pauline, for keeping me company on my cellular phone while I walked my dog, Toby. I must not forget the person who bought me my first typewriter so that I could begin my love of writing. Thanks, Mom.

Prelude

Jane lay on the soft furry white rug that was tossed over the stacks of hay. She felt slightly chilled by the night air as it made its way into the barn and through her lace robe. Goose bumps were multiplying on her naked skin. In the name of art, she whispered to herself. Glancing over at the canvas across from her, she smiled excited. This was the last night that she would have to pose. Her husband's gift was about to be finished.

The coldness that chilled her body could not stop her mind from thinking warm thoughts about her husband. He was such a powerful man in the city where they lived, but when he was with her, alone, he was the most tender man, almost to the point of seeming weak and needy. His touch was sensitive and loving. After ten years of marriage, they were still able to excite each other. Keeping the energy flowing in their relationship was important to both of them.

This gift would keep that fire lit. Never would he expect such a daring piece of art. Richard loved paintings, and this she knew would please him. It was true that no one else would ever see the painting besides the artist, herself, and her husband, but that would make it all the more special. As a couple, she and her husband would share the secret of this painting that was for their eyes only.

The crickets chirping reminded her that she had a long trip home. The distance from the city to the country was one of the sacrifices she was making for this present, but it seemed a small price to pay for the happiness that it would bring her husband. Jane loved giving him surprises.

The barn door creaked a bit. "I was getting a little worried about you," she called out towards the doorway.

Suddenly, the door slammed open and she screamed. The man looked angry and crazed.

Quickly, she covered her body with her shirt. "Get out!"

He held up a video camera. "I'm going to show the whole city what a slut the mayor's wife is."

Anger replaced her fear for her safety. This man had come to ruin her husband's political life by making her out to be some scandalous hussy.

Jane hurried to put her clothes on. "You're crazy," she screamed.

He moved closer to her. His laugh was loud and wicked. "Wait until everyone finds out what you're really like."

Jane saw him drop something on ground at his feet: a knife. He ran towards her. She ran around the stacks of hay and towards the doorway. The man was within arm's reach of her the whole time, but his camera action kept him from touching her. He pulled the camera away and ran ahead of her, pulling the door shut. She reached down and picked up the knife. In her panic, something had gone wrong. The knife, her weapon of protection, was now slicing deep into her stomach.

Seconds felt like hours. She was consciously aware of the dirt, how it smelled, and how cool and moist it was against her skin. With what energy she had left, Jane crawled to her car. Staggering, she had made it to a standing position. Jane pulled the knife from her stomach and let it fall to the ground. Her vision was now blurry and her mind hazy. Someone was watching her as she struggled to get into her car and drive away.

CHAPTER 1

▼

HIRED

Richard moved closer towards the door of Nancy's small apartment. He had talked her into accepting his offer, and he knew it.

"So, you're saying, you want my help," she said with her hands on her hips.

"No, Nancy, I'm telling you that I'll pay you, and you'll have work."

"But, Richard, I don't need any work. I told you, I'm going to be back at the newspaper soon."

"When birds stop flying. Come on. I don't mean to make you feel bad, sweetheart, but this strike is going to outlast your life expectancy. *The Doverlaine Daily* is not going to budge."

Nancy, the thirty-year-old editor, reached out and took hold of the pile of newspaper clippings, copies of public court records, and notes that Richard Fellow was holding out to her. "Fine, I'll do it, but remember, this is a favor for you, not me."

"Fine, Fine." He smiled at her. The tall, stout, forty-five-year-old man who was once the mayor of the city, winked at her. Richard wore his black hair slicked back.

Nancy noticed that his moustache was mostly gray. He must dye his hair she thought. She heard him mumble something.

"What?"

"My publisher said three months or the deal's off. I'd do it myself, but I'm too close to it. Anytime, I think of Jane in that…"

Nancy saw him utterly turn pale. "No, Richard. It's okay. I understand."

"Great. Well, I'll be off. When I get back from my trip, I'll stop by to see how you're doing. Everything you need to complete the manuscript is in that pile. You shouldn't need anything else, but if you do, here's the number to reach me."

Nancy accepted his business card and hugged him good-bye. "You have a safe trip."

"Whoa, I almost forgot." He reached into his pocket and pulled out some bills. "Here's a thousand. I'll pay you another four when you're finished."

"Richard, I can wait."

"Think nothing of it. The publisher gave me an advance."

Nancy wondered how much of an advance, but she didn't ask. She also wondered what he was being paid for the manuscript but wasn't about to ask that either. It was hard to ask a man whose wife had been brutally murdered how much he was going to be paid for writing about her tragic death. What made Richard sign a contract to write such a book in the first place? Was he honestly that broke? How would he handle the publicity that would develop from the book? She grimaced after he had left, realizing that the root of all evil had found its next two victims.

Dumping the newspaper clippings, the copies of the court documents and his notes onto her dinning room table, she cursed the newspaper strike. If she had still been working, she would have had the perfect excuse of being too busy to accept the gruesome job, nor would she have needed Richard's money.

The time was two o'clock in the afternoon, and she had nothing better to do, so she jumped right to work, reading Richard's twenty pages of notes and the fifteen newspaper clippings. The accounts of the events in every article were nearly identical. Only the tragic and upsetting headlines were different: "Missing Woman Found Butchered to Death," "Christian Woman Slain," "Mayor's Wife Murdered," "Mother of Two Found Murdered."

Richard's notes were weak. They were summaries taken from the newspaper articles. There were twenty pages worth of writing in large print, triple spaced, and one sided. It was the kind of writing teachers received from students who were trying to bluff their way through book reports.

"Damn you, Richard. How am I to create a manuscript from such elemental notes?" She slammed her fist down on her dining room table and cursed *The Doverlaine Daily* again.

The doorbell rang sending instant relief to Nancy's nerves. "I'm coming."

A smile spread across her face as she drew her friend into her apartment. "Oh, Claudia, I'm so glad to see you."

Claudia set her large wooden signs down on top of the pile of papers on the dining room table.

"Where were you today?"

"Here."

"Here? You were supposed to be picketing that sucking company that gave our jobs away. Union, my ass! What damn good are they when they can't even save our jobs?"

Claudia was large boned and just a tad overweight. She wore her medium blond hair styled neatly on top of her head. Blue eyes, thick lips and big teeth, gave her a bold handsome appearance.

Nancy in contrast had a more delicate look. She was small boned, slender, and her face had well defined cheekbones, fragile chin, and soft brown eyes.

"I'll make us something to eat. Are you hungry?"

"Starved. This sign is heavy." Claudia pointed to the sign on top of the others that read, *Give Us Back Our Jobs, You Cheap Cheating Slobs.* "I walked in so many circles in front of that damn door that I was dizzy by the time the police arrived."

"Police?"

"Yeah. They arrested Jimmy Thortoon, you know, the guy who always asked you out."

"Yeah, so what happened? Did he throw a rock at one of the windows or something?"

"No. It was my fault. I yelled out something rotten, and then I threw my banana peel at the scabs. You know how I have such bad luck. The peel hit this, I swear to you, ten-foot guy square in his face. The dude must have weighed a thousand pounds. He started hollering and grabbing at us. He got hold of Jimmy's shirt collar, just strangling him. If the police hadn't stepped in, I think Jimmy would have died."

"Did Jimmy see you throw the banana peel?"

"I don't know, but even if he did, he's not going to remember. After the way that guy was shaking him, he'll be lucky to remember his name."

Nancy checked her refrigerator one more time. "Claudia, I have bad news and good news and then more bad news. I'm out of food that we would want to eat, but I have money, and we can go out to eat. While we're eating, I'll tell you the bad news."

"I have bad news and good news too. I'm too tired to move off of your couch, and my feet hurt. If you have our food delivered, you can tell me your bad news sooner."

"Fine, I'll order it from that Greek place around the corner. While I'm looking for that carry-out menu I brought home last month, you can read something."

Nancy removed the picket signs from the dining room table and scooped up the newspaper clippings, the copies of the court documents, and Richard's notes. She handed them to Claudia and frantically hunted for that menu.

Claudia recognized the article that she had written. "This one's mine. Damn, I wish I still had my job at the paper. I did such terrific work, didn't I? My work was the best. We won that award last year because of my work. Remember?"

"Yes, of course, I do. And yes, your work is terrific. Now, please stand up before your head swells more and becomes too heavy to lift."

"What are you doing?"

"I think that menu is under the couch cushion."

Nancy raised the cushion, but the space was bare. "Go ahead and sit back down. I'm going to look in the cat's toy box."

"Why? Does Fee Fee order out?"

"No, silly, he orders in, and his name's not Fee Fee, it's Clansy."

"Why do you have all of these articles about Jane Fellow's murder?"

"Read those papers," Nancy yelled out as she headed into another room.

Seconds later, Nancy ran back into the living room. "I found it!"

"Great, let me have it."

Nancy handed Claudia the menu. "Did you read his notes?"

"Are those her husband's notes?"

"Yes, he wants me to write a book about her murder. I don't know how I'm going to write it from those puny notes of his. Aren't they pathetic? His wife is brutally murdered and his response is, 'I felt bad.' Isn't that awful? I mean a person feels bad about breaking a good piece of china, but for a spouse's death, a person ought to feel pain stricken, heart broken, debilitated."

"Unless he didn't love her."

"Oh, that's silly, of course, he loved her."

"How do you know?"

"I don't know, I just do. What are you going to order?"

"I want a gyro with heavy sauce and double onions, fries and a large Greek salad. We can split it and some pita bread. Listen, you know what's weird? About a week ago, I was over at Sally's, and she had a bunch of old newspaper clippings about Jane's murder."

"Why?"

"I don't know. I sort of saw them by accident."

"Accident?"

"She was busy doing something, and I got bored. You know how I am when I'm bored."

"Yeah, Snoopy. Hmmm, I wonder what Sally was doing with them. Maybe you could tell her you glanced around and saw them, and you could tell her that you're curious about why she had them."

"I don't think so. They were inside of a shoebox buried beneath a bunch of junk inside of a drawer."

"You're disgusting."

"No, I'm not. Now order our food. Hurry up because I have a date tonight."

"With who?"

"The police officer that arrested Jimmy asked me to the movies."

"No!"

"Yes. Oh, and is he ever gorgeous. Hot. Hot. Hot. Dark wavy hair and a body like the Rock."

Nancy pulled the phone away from her ear. "Read the notes, Claudia, or I'm not ordering you any food."

"I'm reading. Don't forget to say extra sauce and onions."

Claudia read quickly through the notes and then handed them back to Nancy. "Yeah, this is weak. Richard Fellow is a jerk."

"I know that. How am I going to write something decent from that?"

"What is he paying you, and why does he want you to write about his wife's murder?"

"I don't know. He said that a publisher wanted the story, and that he's doing it for personal reasons."

"Which are?"

"He didn't say."

"Then, you must know it's financial reasons. He must be getting paid a bloody fortune for it."

"I don't know. He's paying me five thousand. One up front."

"Why are you doing it?"

Nancy picked up the picket signs. "Duh."

"I know, but must you grovel?"

"Watch it, I'm feeding you."

"Why doesn't he write it himself?"

"He said that he was too close to it."

CHAPTER 2

▼

DEBT

After Claudia left, Nancy dove into the court records. The convicted man was Philip Securd, a twenty-four year-old White male. His DNA and fingerprints were found at the crime scene in the city where the victim's body was found with multiple stab wounds. A witness, Josephine Wilderk, placed him at the crime scene at 8:00 p.m. Her testimony was a quick read. Philip did not take the witness stand. The prosecution accused him of leaving Denten town where he lived, going into the city, and stabbing the mayor's wife to death. No motive given. Philip's lawyer did not contest to the accusations. There was not much of anything from the defense.

Nancy kept thinking about what Claudia had said about Sally having the same newspaper clippings of Jane's murder. Hours later, she succumbed to her curiosity and phoned Sally.

"Hi, how are you? Yes, I heard Jimmy got arrested. Claudia told me all about it. Yes, that's what she said; some big guy grabbed Jimmy up and just started shaking him for no reason. That's the kind of behavior one can expect from a scab." Nancy made herself comfortable on the couch. Clansy curled up next to her. She switched the phone to her other ear so that she could pet him.

"Guess who visited me today? No, I meant besides Claudia. It was Richard Fellow, our ex-mayor."

"I thought you liked him. Well, then why did you just refer to him as a big idiot? He what? He paid you a hundred dollars to write a twenty-page summary from the news articles about his wife's murder? He said that he was too close to the event to write about it? Yes, that does make sense. But it does seem to me that an interview with him would have been in order, you know, to get his personal experience recorded."

Clansy leaped from Nancy's lap as she shot up. "He's being paid fifty thousand dollars? He only offered you five thousand to write the manuscript? Of course, I can see why you turned it down. Did he tell you that he was being paid that much from the publisher? I see. No, you did the right thing. I would have called the publisher too if I had a friend working there. You're right, only an idiot would accept his offer. No, that's okay, I understand. I have something to do too. Right, I'll talk to you later. Take care."

"Too close to it!" Nancy looked into the mirror on the wall across from her. "You idiot! He's being paid fifty thousand dollars, and you're only getting five, and you're going to do all of the work."

Nancy checked her pocket for Richard's business card. Then, she checked the top of the dining room table, under the couch, and everywhere else. It was nearly midnight when she found his business card under the throw rug, under the dining room table. She rested on the couch and fell asleep.

Pleasant dreams soon turned ugly with the day's reading material still fresh in her memory. She saw herself running through an alley being chased by a huge dark shadowy figure. A gleaming sharp blade of a huge knife was reaching out for her throat. Trapped by large brick buildings, she had no place else to run. There was nothing else she could do but scream.

In the morning, Nancy woke up vaguely remembering her dream. While the details were missing, the chilling feeling stayed with her. She placed Richard's business card next to the phone. That would be the first order of business to take care of right after breakfast.

Nancy found a package of cinnamon Pop-tarts in the cupboard and had them with her coffee. At ten o'clock, a bill collector called her to discuss her credit card balance. After she hung up the phone in disgust, it rang again, and this time it was her landlord calling to discuss her rent. Her thousand dollars was already being spent. Quickly, before another unpleasant person phoned her, she phoned Richard's business number.

"Richard, I. I'm fine thank you. No, I'm not finished." She laughed along with him. "I wanted to tell you that I. Yes, I know that you appreciate what I'm doing for you. Please, Richard, quit thanking me. Another five thousand? Okay, Richard. Yes, I was just checking on you to make sure that you had arrived safely. Yes, I will. You have fun too. Bye."

Clansy leaped into her lap. "Clansy, you poor cat. Your owner is a weakling. Why didn't I tell him?"

The orange and white striped cat leaped to the floor and walked over to his empty food bowl. "Meow."

"Right, you need food; I need food. Bills need to be paid. It's called life."

Nancy thought about where to begin with the book and decided that getting the convicted murderer's story was not a bad idea. She called an acquaintance of hers, Debra Wunderkaieg. Debra worked as a prison guard at the penitentiary where Philip Securd was being held.

CHAPTER 3

▼

FELON

Debra was a large muscular African American woman. In her prison guard uniform, she was intimidating. She unlocked the gate letting Nancy into the prison. "Come on in, girl. I don't know why you'd want to talk to any of this garbage, but come on. Don't stop in front of any of their cells. They'll try to grab you. Just keep moving."

The place was gray and dingy, cement floors, steel bars, absolutely a hideous place to live. A strong putrid odor and a nauseating cleanser smell took turns controlling the area where the men's cells were.

Nancy looked through the bars at Philip Secured. She knew that he was twenty-five years old, but he looked far older than that. His complexion was pasty white and his body was so thin. Beneath his sandy brown stringy hair, were the saddest brown eyes that she had ever seen. He had been in prison for one year already.

The garbage, as Debra had called the prisoners, were yelling obscenities, and some men were begging her to stand in front of their cells. Some were clanking objects against their bars; others were loudly hooting and whistling. The plan to interview Philip and get his story about the night of the murder was not working, as she had visualized.

"Um, Philip, my name is Nancy." She made eye contact with him. "I'm writing a book for a friend about the murder that you were convicted of. I'd like to have your side of the story." It occurred to her that she was yelling and that Philip would have to do the same. This interview was never going to work.

Frustrated, she yelled out, "This is my tape recorder. I'm going to leave it with you and these two tapes. If you could just put your story on them and then give the tapes to Guard Wunderkaieg, I'll include your story in the book."

Philip took the tape-recorder. He turned it over and examined it carefully.

"You can keep the tape recorder," she added.

He threw his head back and began laughing. Then, he stopped as abruptly as he had started. He tilted his head down and began crying.

Nancy thought to herself, don't feel sorry for him. He hacked someone to death. Don't feel sorry for him. He deserves to be here. He's dangerous.

"Well, I'll just be going now." Nancy saw Debra down the aisle way. She was standing in front of one of the cells yelling at a prisoner.

Philip stopped crying and rushed a step forward. He grabbed Nancy's hand pulling it towards him and through the bars.

Nancy stiffened. "Debra," she hollered.

"Thank you," he said softly and let go of her hand.

Debra ran to her. "What'd he do?" she demanded.

"Nothing, I'm ready to leave."

Nancy was at first chilled by the thought of him touching her, but that was her mind's reaction. What followed was a strange feeling. Philip's touch had been gentle unlike what she had expected from a cold-blooded murderer.

CHAPTER 4

▼

FRIEND

"Thanks for coming over, Claudia."

"No problem. What's up?"

"I called Sally the other day. I told her that Richard had stopped in to see me. You're not going to believe this, but she told me that he paid her a hundred dollars to write that summary."

"I believe it. That explains why it's so awful."

Well, he even offered her five thousand dollars to write the manuscript. Can you believe that? He had already asked her. That's why you saw those newspaper clippings in her house. They were the same ones that he gave to me. And, wait until you hear this. She called his publisher. Luckily, a friend of hers worked for the guy. Sally found out that he was being paid fifty thousand dollars for the manuscript that he asked her to write."

"The one that you're writing now?"

"Right."

"You big dummy."

"I know."

"Call Richard and tell him that you won't do it."

"I did. I mean, I tried to. He offered me another five thousand, and I couldn't say no."

"What?"

"Well, I had a bill collector and my landlord on my back just before I talked with him, and he kept thanking me for helping him, and I don't know how it happened. I just heard myself saying thank you and well, I'm stuck."

"You're stupid."

"That too."

"You know what your problem is; it's that you're weak. It's not your fault. It comes from being pampered like a spoiled brat when you were a kid. Now, you're living on your own, and you've got no one to do your bidding for you. You're not used to doing things by yourself. If you'd grown up like me, practically changing your own diapers, you'd be strong and independent."

"Oh."

"Really. You'd probably write better too."

"What?"

"You're always worried about hurting someone's feelings. Your articles always sound like fairy tales with happy endings."

"No, they don't."

"Where's your portfolio?"

"I don't have one."

"Yeah, right."

"I don't."

"All writers and editors keep copies of their work."

"I don't."

Claudia glanced around the living room and walked directly over to Nancy's bookshelf. "Then, what's this?" she asked pulling the large book from the shelf.

"It's my scrapbook."

"See, no one pulls anything over on me. I can see through people just like looking through a glass of water."

Claudia sat down next to Nancy on the couch and opened the scrapbook. "Listen to this. Plant closes after fourteen years. Thousands lose their jobs, but many are optimistic that they will find work in a new plant. Optimistic! Who would believe that? There wasn't another plant for a thousand miles around that place, and entrepreneurs were only interested in building toxic wells in it. Here, listen to this one. Local woman and Olympic contender breaks her leg just before the big race. She says, she'll be looking forward to the next Olympic games. Nancy, everyone knew she wouldn't be in another Olympic race after that. Her leg was broken in six places. The doctors said that she was lucky to walk."

"So?"

"So, you sugarcoat everything."

"Give me my scrapbook." Nancy yanked it from her.

"I'm sorry."

"No, you're not."

"Yes, I am. I didn't mean to hurt your feelings. That's one of my problems. I have a big mouth."

"That's true."

"Feel better?"

"Not yet."

"I can't keep a boyfriend. I'm overweight. Every day's a bad hair-day."

"I feel better. Now, stop."

"You know, what I can't figure out, Nancy, is why Richard asked Sally to write that summary. She's not an editor. She's not even a writer. She was the coffee girl for crying out loud."

"No, she wasn't. She was an apprentice."

"She wasn't."

"She was."

"She never wrote anything."

"You never gave her the chance."

"She made great coffee. That was the reason I visited her last week. I missed her coffee."

"That's not nice."

"I'm kidding. I had to pick up some flyers from her house, but the coffee was delicious."

"You should have given her a chance to write for you at the newspaper."

"Her summary was terrible. You said so yourself."

"Yeah, well, look what Richard gave her to work with. I'm having difficulty myself. But, guess what I've decided to do? Instead of using all this old stuff, I'm going to write the manuscript based on fresh interviews from the criminal and the witnesses."

"Ingenuity, that's where you make up for your sugarcoating. You always did have the best ideas on the staff."

"Thank you."

"You're welcome. Now, where are you at on this manuscript?"

"Yesterday, I dropped off a tape recorder to Philip Secured. I was going to interview him, but the prison was too disgusting. Those creeps kept banging on the bars and calling me names. They were trying to touch me. It gave me the willies."

"I'm surprised, you even went in."

"I was scared to death. Philip touched me, grabbed my hand through the bars. Anyway, I gave him my tape recorder and asked him to give the tapes to a guard that I know."

"That was smart."

"Today, I'm going to set up interviews with the witnesses."

"Where are you taking your list of witnesses from?"

"I have the witness list that the police used for their investigation; then there are the court documents, and the news articles. I have plenty of information."

"You know that some of the witnesses didn't get to testify in court."

"I know, that's why I'm using the list from the police station."

"Good."

"You know, Claudia, you could work with me on this."

"Nope, I can't. Someone has to represent our grievances. I'm in charge of the picket line today, and I have to help pass out more flyers begging people to refuse to buy the newspaper being produced by those scabs."

"Are you mad at me for not picketing?"

"No, because I know you'll feed me. So, what's for lunch today?"

CHAPTER 5

▼

WITNESS

Nancy walked up the long pathway to Mr. Nec's house. He lived in the country, but he was in the city on the night of the murder. While the murder was reported to have taken place in the big city at eight o'clock p.m., Mr. Nec's police report was in contrast to that fact.

A pot-bellied, silver-haired man opened the door and smiled at her. Nancy smiled back. "Mr. Nec?"

"You, the little girl I spoke to on the phone?"

"That's right, and thank you so much for giving me this interview."

"Come on in. Ethel will fetch you a glass of her homemade lemonade."

Ethel had short curly ash brown hair, a long face, and big hazel eyes. She was also wearing a long cotton dress.

After a glass of lemonade and a few homemade ginger cookies, Mr. Nec began to tell his eyewitness story. He leaned back in his chair and took a deep breath. Then, he let it out slowly. "I was in the city 'cause my sister was gettin married. She's too old. I told her, but she never had any sense."

Ethel entered the living room and sat next to Nancy on the couch. She smiled warmly.

"They're gettin divorced too. I tried to warn her. She wants what Ethel and I got, but we been married forty-five years, an ya can't do that overnight."

Nancy smiled. "Forty-five years, that's nice."

He cleared his voice. "Ethel, fetch me another lemonade. You want some more?"

"No, I'm fine, thank you." Nancy watched Ethel jump right up, take his glass, and rush off to the kitchen.

"Now, I was visitin my sister. She was gettin married to Ted, a man who wanted her money. I told her, but she never has any sense. The reception was boring, so I went for a drive."

"At what time?"

"It was exactly nine o'clock. I remember looking at my watch. I drove up to this little store for some cigars. Eh, Ethel, fetch me one ah my cigars."

Ethel jumped up from her seat, rushed out of the room, and ran back in again with a cigar. She tore open the wrapper and handed it to him.

He gave her a look of disgust. "Ethel, what good is my cigar if you don't get me the lighter?"

"Oh, oh, ho, ho," she laughed and ran off to get the lighter.

He shook his head. "I think she's gettin senile."

Once he had his cigar lit, the room full of smoke, and Nancy coughing, he continued. "I saw this blue car drive up, a Cutlass. This woman got out. She looked beat up. Her lip was bleedin and she was cryin. She tried to tell me somethin."

"Where were you?"

"I was on my way into the store. She grabbed my arm. Show her Ethel, how she grabbed me. Ethel knows 'cause I showed her a bunch a times."

Ethel quickly grabbed Nancy's left arm and gave it a tight squeeze. She looked over to her husband.

"Yank it up a bit, Ethel. There, that's about how she grabbed me. Then, she shoved me a bit."

Nancy braced herself, but then relaxed when Mr. Nec yelled to his wife to let her arm go. She rubbed her arm for a second and resumed writing in her notebook.

"She said, 'I need help' and she said that over an over. Her voice was kinda high. Ethel, talk in that high voice that you can do. You know the one you do when you're tryin to sound like the minister's wife."

Ethel smiled. In a high voice she said, "Let's give the choir a big hand brothers an sisters."

"Ethel, say what that woman said," he ordered.

"I need help."

"No, Ethel, not in your voice. In that high voice."

Ethel finally performed to her husband's satisfaction. He smiled. "There, that's how she sounded. Just like that."

"Mr. Nec, what happened next?"

"She fell on me. I had to hold her up. Ethel…"

"Mr. Nec, I understand."

"Good. Ethel, fetch me my slippers."

Nancy let out a sigh. Ethel sprang up to fetch his slippers.

"I held her. Then this man drove up in a white pickup truck. Ugly color for a pickup. Red or blue's 'bout the only good colors for a pickup."

"What did the man look like?"

"Tall an thin. He had a hood on. Some sort a joggin outfit. It was shiny black. He had a mustache. That's 'bout all I can remember 'bout him. He took her an left."

"Took her?"

"Drug her into the truck an drove off."

"What did you do?"

"I went into the store an told the man behind the counter, an he called the cops."

"Then what happened?"

"The cops came an arrested me for drivin drunk. I'd had some beers at the reception, a couple shots, but I was fine."

"What about the woman?"

"The cops told me they'd look for her, but they didn't believe me. They thought I made it up. I told um she got out of that blue car. Couple days later, two cops from the city came to my house an wanted to know what I saw that night at the store. I told um again, an this time they was listenin, but it was too late. On the news, they'd already said that she was murdered."

"Do you know why your testimony wasn't used at the trial?"

"What I said didn't match up to what the cops found. Somethin 'bout the time not bein right, an they said my bein drunk at the time wouldn't do the man any good."

"The man, do you mean Philip Secured?"

"Yeah. It was his lawyer that didn't want to use me."

"Are you sure that the woman you saw and held that night was Jane Fellow?"

"Oh, yeah. It was her. When they showed her picture on the news, I told Ethel. Didn't I, Ethel? I said Ethel, that's the woman that was in the store parking lot the night I got arrested."

Ethel nodded her head enthusiastically. Nancy closed her notebook and handed Mr. Nec a release form. "This is just in case I use your report in the book. I'm not certain that it will be used."

"Why not?" he asked sounding offended.

"Oh, I'll use it. I meant, sometimes the publisher tightens things up a bit and cuts stuff down and might delete something."

"Ethel, fetch me my pen."

"Here," Nancy said quickly, handing him hers."

"No, no, no, I have to use my pen. Ethel knows that. Hurry up, Ethel."

After he signed the form, he held on to it. "Am I gonna be paid anything?"

"No."

"Oh." He held the form out to her. She raised her arm to take it, but he pulled it away before she could grasp it.

"Ya see, I asked 'cause no one gave me nothin last time. I didn't testify, so they didn't pay me anything, an I was out twenty dollars 'cause of it."

"Twenty dollars?"

"That's what my shirt cost."

"Your shirt?"

"The one that got blood on it. I told ya, I had to hold on to her."

"Did you tell the police that you had a shirt with her blood on it?"

"They didn't ask, but I told that defense lawyer, an he said to throw it away."

"What?"

"Oh, I didn't. Those kinda shirts absorb like the devil. They make good rags."

"You still have it?"

"Maybe. If I do, it's out in the garage."

"If you have it, I'll buy it from you."

"He leaned forward in his chair. "Fer what?"

"Oh, I'd just like to have it."

"Fer what?"

"Fer what?" she repeated.

"Fer what price?" he asked sounding agitated.

"Oh. What do you want for it?"

"I want what I paid fer it."

"Absolutely, Mr. Nec. That's not a problem."

"Ethel, don't just sit there, Honey. Ya heard us talkin. Get up an go find that shirt." He leaned back in his chair.

"Ethel, would you like some help?" Nancy asked.

Ethel accepted her offer, and the two women went into the garage where there were no vehicles just boxes, bags, and shelves full of junk. They searched through six bags marked RAGS on them. The rags were old clothes that were still dirty.

"Aaahhh!" Nancy screamed realizing that she had touched a pair of Mr. Nec's old stained underwear. She flung them across the garage and kept beating her hand against her thigh as though she could detach it from her. "Ethel, I think we better dump these rags out, and this might go a little faster."

As they dumped the rags onto the floor, Ethel hand searched them while Nancy scanned them with her eyes. Ethel spotted the shirt and picked it up. "It smells bad. I could wash it for you."

"No, no thank you."

At arm's-length, Nancy held the white shirt that stank of perhaps stale beer and body odor. She was not going to try and detect exactly what it was that she smelled. It had a few orange dots and two long orange streaks on the front of it. The armpit areas were stained yellow.

CHAPTER 6

▼

EYEWITNESS

The following day, Nancy drove into the bad neighborhood where Josephine Wilderk lived. Many of the buildings had gang graffiti painted on them. Garbage was scattered across the yards and into the roads. Fences were damaged. Windows were boarded or barred for protection. She cautiously made her way up to the small gray, rundown house. Sweat trickled down her face. The June weather was hot and humid. Nancy rang the doorbell.

The door opened a crack, and a woman's voice boomed through. "Who are you?"

"I'm Nancy Mead. I phoned you earlier. I know you said that you didn't want to talk with me, but I really need your story for this book."

"Go away or I'll call the cops."

"It's just a short interview, only a few questions, really. Please."

"I'm calling the cops."

The door slammed shut. Nancy yelled out, "I'll pay you for your time."

The door opened wider than before. "How much?"

"You tell me."

"A hundred dollars."

"A hundred dollars?" Nancy checked her purse. She still had a few hundred from the advance Richard had given her. "That's fine."

The door swung open. "Come on in," Josephine called out as she moved farther into the house.

Cautiously, Nancy approached the door. Her persistence was an asset to her job, but a fine line existed between the art of persuasion and the act of harassment. It was easy to cross that line without knowing that you had. Slowly, she pushed the door fully open and looked into the house.

Josephine was sitting at the dining room table blowing her nose on a handkerchief. Her brunette hair was straggly and dull, and her arms and legs were unnaturally thin, anorexic looking. The woman was shaking. Her living room was bare. There were only two wooden kitchen chairs and a rickety old table in the kitchen.

"Sit down. What do you want to know?" She asked irritated.

Nancy studied Josephine's blood shot eyes hoping to find a tad bit of politeness. Her image did not match up with her appearance in court when she was a witness on the stand. She had been described as a wholesome contented housewife with five children.

"Are your children out playing?"

"What children?" Josephine snapped.

"You don't have children?"

"Oh, yeah, I do." She paused. "They live with their fathers."

"I thought you were married?"

"Never. Well, once. It was a mistake."

"Oh, I see. So, when you took the stand in Securd's case, you weren't married, and you didn't have any children living with you?"

"No. Is this what you wanted to know?"

"No. I wanted to know what you saw the night that Securd murdered Jane Fellow."

"Blood, lots of blood. Anything else you want to know?"

"When did it happen?"

"The night he did it."

"Do you really want the hundred dollars?"

"I'm talking with you aren't I?"

"I need details."

"Fine. Do you have a report or something of what I said on the stand? I need to refresh my memory."

"No."

"All right, let me think. I was at a friend's, and we heard some screaming going on. I wanted to phone the cops, but the phone wasn't working, so I went outside to see what was happening. There was this alley a couple yards away, and I saw the shadows of two people, a woman and a man. The man had a knife, and he was cutting her up. That was it."

"What did the screams sound like?"

"They were deep."

"Not high?"

"No, low. There were three of them and that was it."

"You didn't say that they were low on the witness stand."

"You said that you didn't have a report about what I said."

"I do have one, but not with me."

"The lawyers didn't ask me what the screams sounded like. Are you finished?"

"All you saw were shadows?"

"That's it."

"You didn't hear any voices talking?"

"Just the screams."

"How did you know that it was Philip Secured?"

"Same height."

"In court, you said that you actually saw him."

"If I said that, then I did."

"But, you just told me that you only saw shadows."

"It didn't happen yesterday. Let me think. I did see him. He stumbled backwards out of the alley a bit, and I saw the back of him."

"Is that all?"

"If you're done, I am."

"No, I mean, is that all that you saw of him, just the back of him?"

"I know the back of someone's head when I see it. He was the same height, same hair color, same head shape. What the hell else do you need? The monster had his fingerprints all over everything. He even had his blood at the scene, BNA everywhere."

"You mean DNA."

"BNA, DNA, what the hell does it matter? That monster was there, and he did it."

"Okay, calm down."

"Are you done?"

"Yes." Nancy pulled a hundred dollar bill from her purse and paid Josephine.

CHAPTER 7

▼

PHILIP'S STORY

Nancy arrived home and checked her mailbox. There was a small package for her from Debra Wunderkaieg. She quickly opened it, and as she had expected, it contained the two tiny tapes. All she had to do was purchase a new micro cassette recorder so that she could hear them.

Right now, she just wanted to go swimming. It was a hot sticky day, and Josephine's rude, obnoxious attitude had made the day completely uncomfortable. A nice swim Nancy hoped would wash all the unpleasantness away. She packed the sunscreen, the coconut suntan lotion, her swimsuit, and favorite beach towel, the one with Snoopy on it, and she drove to the public pool at the park.

It was useless, no matter how many times she entered the water, she always came back out thinking about what was on the two tiny tapes in her apartment. "That's it," she uttered and began packing her pool items.

The stop she made before reaching home was to a store to purchase the micro cassette recorder. Her money was spending fast. She had to use a credit card. Luckily, she still had one that had at least fifty dollars worth of credit still left on it.

As soon as she entered her apartment, she sat down at her dining room table and listened to Securd's story. His voice sounded anxious. "I didn't do it. I keep telling everybody that, but they won't listen to me. I never murdered that woman. I'd never hurt anybody. I didn't do it. I wasn't ever there at that place where she was killed. That night that they said I did it, I was at home. I was by myself. I lived in a garage behind these nice people's house, the Portsons. They let me stay there when I was 18. I used to live with the Petersons. And, before that, it was the Lakes. And, before that, it was the Williams. And, before that, I can't remember. But, I never had to live in an orphanage. They said, my mother died when I was a baby. I'd always been taken in by somebody. Always stayed with them until they couldn't keep me anymore. Some places were nicer than others. Finally, I got my own place behind the Portsons' house. I lived in their garage. It was nice."

Nancy turned the volume up on the recorder. The anxiety had disappeared from his voice, and now he sounded calmer. "I had this job down at the grocery store, bagging groceries at first, and then he let me stock the shelves. And, then I moved up to Second Assistant Manager, and I was put in charge of inventory. It was hard, but I got the hang of it after a couple of weeks, and then the boss gave me a raise after I quit making mistakes. It was a good job, and I worked there for about six years. I walked to work. It was just down the road. I never had a car. I can't get a driver's license. They say I'm not smart enough to pass the test. I asked Dr. Kebler if that was true. He said that I didn't need to waste my time learning to drive. With the short time I have left to live, he said, I shouldn't spend any time worrying about anything. He said I shouldn't do anything but be happy. I don't know if he knows I'm here. I'd like to tell him, I'm not happy."

Nancy stopped the recorder, looked through her purse, and pulled out an ink pen. She took a sheet of paper from the counter and began jotting down notes. She turned the recorder back on.

His voice was beginning to sound shaky again. "I wish I was back home, and I could work at the store again. I used to go fishing on my days off. I'd go fishing at the river. It was only a short ways from my home. I was on my way there that day the police came and told me I had to go with them. They didn't tell me why. They just said that I was a suspect. I didn't know what that meant, but it didn't sound good."

Nancy heard a buzz sound and a loud clank. "It's time for my exercise in the yard." She heard the loud clank again. "I'm back. I ran around the track. I wish they'd let me stay in the yard longer. I get so tired of this little space, that ugly toilet, and these bars. I want to be back home. I was going to get a dog from my neighbors, the Robbins, but the police put me in jail. When I went to court, I never got to say anything. This man that said he was my lawyer did all the talking. The only thing I did was stand up and sit down. I heard them telling lies about me, but my lawyer told me not to get upset and to keep quiet, that we'd get our turn to speak. After court, they put me in prison, and I don't know how long I've been here. I bet I don't have much time left. I wish I could spend the rest of it at home. I'm not happy here."

Nancy turned off the recorder and jotted down some more notes. Then, she turned it back on. "I didn't kill that lady. I was at home on the night that they said I did that. I don't remember your name, but will you help me get out of here? I didn't do what they said I did."

Nancy heard nothing more on the tape. She forwarded it, checked the other side, and scanned through both sides of the second tape, but there was nothing more. Philip's story had ended and left Nancy full of questions.

She began reviewing the court documents again. Hours went by while she searched for answers. The ringing of the doorbell startled her. Nancy jumped up from her chair. Seeing that it was Claudia who had stopped by to visit her, she quickly invited her in and ushered her to a seat at the dining room table. "Oh, thank God you're here. Sit down. I've got so much to tell you."

"I've got something to tell you too."

Claudia sat down in the chair and glanced at the scattered pile of papers on the table. "I see you've been busy."

"You bet I have. Claudia, it's awful. Philip Secured was setup. He didn't do it."

"Didn't do what?"

"He didn't kill Jane Fellow."

Claudia focused on Nancy noticing that her hair was messy, her arms looked dirty, and she smelled like coconuts. "Are you feeling all right?"

"I'm fine. I went to the pool today." Nancy stood up. "Philip Secured is innocent. The witness that said she saw him there in the alley that night didn't see him. She saw shadows of two people. She saw the back of a man's head and that was at night."

"Street lights must have lit him up enough or there wouldn't have been shadows, Nancy. She probably did get a good look at him."

"The back of a man's head! You can't tell who someone is from the back of their head especially if you've never met them before."

"Height, hair color, and head shape, it works for me."

"What?"

"His fingerprints and his blood were found at the scene of the crime."

"I know, but something's not right." Nancy flailed her right arm into the air and began pacing back and forth near Claudia as she talked. "The lawyers painted Josephine Wilderk out to be Susie

Homemaker, and she's not. That Josephine is closer to being a coke freak than a loving mother of five children. They don't even live with her, and she doesn't have any living room furniture. Probably sold it for drugs. She even made me pay her a hundred dollars before she'd talk to me. I'll bet her kids aren't living with their fathers. They're probably all in foster care."

"Pathetic."

"It's worse than that, Claudia. I just listened," Nancy stretched her arm across the table and picked up her cassette recorder, "to Philip Securd, and he doesn't sound like a cold calculating killer. He sounds like an innocent child that doesn't know what's going on. He said his doctor told him that he didn't have long to live. It was never in the court documents that he was sick or anything. These court documents," Nancy picked them up and scrunched them, "make him sound like a healthy normal person, and he's not! These court documents state that Philip worked as a manager at a grocery store and lived in a rented apartment. They don't state that he had been working at the grocery store most of the time as a bag boy, or that he lived in a garage, or that he was mentally slow. And there is definitely no mention of a fatal illness."

Claudia turned her head left, but Nancy had already paced back the other way. "Nancy, stop moving." Claudia stood up and blocked Nancy's path. "Sit down."

Nancy followed her orders.

"What you need to do, Nancy, is to stop getting upset. You need to check out Philip's story. You're a reporter and an editor. It's your job to investigate the story for the truth, not rant and rave and try to convince the world of his innocents. That's a lawyer's job. Here, let me get you some water to drink."

Claudia poured Nancy a tall glass of water and herself one too. "Here, drink this." She reached into her purse and pulled out a bottle of pills and opened them. She took two pills and swallowed them with some water. "Here, Nancy, take these." She handed two small white pills to Nancy.

"What are they?"

"Just over the counter medicine for a headache."

"I'm sorry, Claudia. Did I give you a headache?"

"Yes, but don't be sorry. Here, take them."

"I don't have a headache."

"Open your hand." Claudia placed them in Nancy's hand. "Save them for when you do need them."

Claudia sat down next to her. "Do you feel better?"

"Yes, a little."

"Good." Claudia began straightening the scattered papers, forming a neat pile. She took the court documents and the cassette recorder from Nancy and placed them neatly on top of the pile. Then, she pushed the pile away from Nancy and her until it was at the other end of the table. "There, now, that's better. You've been working too hard on this. You need a break. Did I tell you that Jimmy was in the hospital?"

"Jimmy?"

"Thortoon. You know, the guy at work that used to ask you out all of the time?"

"Yes, I remember him. Who could forget someone so nauseating?"

"Oh, come on, he's not that bad. Besides, the poor guy had a broken collarbone and a fractured jaw. He just got out of the hospital a couple of days ago. He's still pretty sore."

"What happened to him?"

"I told you, he was beaten up by that scab worker."

"You told me, he was arrested, not injured."

"I didn't know that he was, but when I found out, I felt awful."

"You should have. You're the one that caused it."

"I know that, so I went to visit him. All he wanted to do was talk about you."

"Well, I'm glad that I didn't go to visit him. I feel sorry for him, but I really can't stand him. He makes my skin crawl. I don't know why, but I just never liked him. Maybe it's because he was always pestering me."

"Nancy, you're not making this easy for me."

"What's wrong?"

"You're my friend, right?"

"Of course."

"Well, I have a problem."

"What is it? I'll help you, Claudia."

"I felt guilty about what I did to Jimmy, and when I was visiting him, he asked me…well, he asked me," she finished it quickly, "if I could get you to go out with him."

"No."

"Yes."

"No!"

"One date?"

"No."

"It's one little itty bitty date."

"No."

"It's not going to ruin your life. You're not marrying the guy. Please!"

"No."

"You said, you would help me."

"I didn't know what you wanted."

"Please, I'll never ask you for anything again."

"I know you won't because I'm going to kill you first." Nancy looked at her friend's pleading eyes. "When is the date?"

Claudia smiled. "Oh, thank you."

"Well, when is it, Claudia?"

"Tonight."

"You're kidding?"

"He's taking you to the movies and then to dinner."

"Then you're coming too. We can double."

"No, that won't work. I'm still seeing the policeman that arrested Jimmy."

"I don't want to do this."

"Look at it this way. You're getting a free movie and a free meal."

"Don't. It's not free."

"I'm sorry."

"You better be."

Claudia glanced at her watch. "I better get going. You need some time to get ready. He's picking you up in an hour. I didn't know it was this late already."

Claudia gave Nancy a hug good-bye. "Look at it this way; you needed a break."

"This isn't a break, and you know it. He's a nut."

"I'm really thankful that you're helping me out."

"Good-bye, Claudia."

"You're not mad at me are you?"

"Good-bye, Claudia."

After Claudia left, Nancy returned to the dining room table and picked up her glass of water. Now, she had a headache. She swallowed the two aspirin in one gulp.

CHAPTER 8

▼

DENTEN

Nancy's wheels were spinning dust into the fresh country air as she drove down the peaceful dirt roads. She had driven past a gas station, a church, and a bar before coming to the road that Philip Securd used to live on. There were only three houses on the road and farther down, a small grocery store. The Portsons lived in a large white farm styled house, and in the backyard was a medium sized garage, and to the right of that, a red barn.

Nancy stood on the long porch and knocked once on the front door. An elderly woman with white hair that was neatly pulled back into a bun answered immediately. She had a gentle face and kind eyes. Smiling, she stood before Nancy in her dress and apron.

"Come in. We're so glad that you could make it, Ms. Staples. Please, come in."

Nancy was already inside the house and seated on the couch before she had the chance to clear up her mistaken identity. "I'm not Ms. Staples."

"You're not from the real-estate office?"

"No. I'm sorry. I'm not. I'm Nancy Mead. I'm writing a book for a friend, and I wanted to find out where Philip Securd lived."

"We can't help you. You'll have to leave."

"But, Mrs. Portson, I want to help Philip."

"You do?"

"Who's here?" asked an elderly tall man with gray hair. He was on his way into the living room wheeling a walker in front of him.

Mrs. Portson walked over to her husband and hollered at him. "She's not from the real-estate, Ed. She says she wants to help Philip."

He shook his head. "Poor Philip. How's he doing?"

"Well, he's…unhappy."

"What?" Mr. Portson yelled.

Nancy repeated much louder, "He's unhappy."

Mr. Portson looked over to his wife. "What'd she say?"

"She said that Philip's unhappy." After Mrs. Portson yelled at her husband, she turned to Nancy. "Dear, you have to yell at him. His hearing aid's broke, and the new one's not going to be here until tomorrow."

"Okay, I will."

"What's she saying now?"

With quite a bit of yelling Nancy had made it to the door of the garage where Philip used to live. Mrs. Portson explained that Philip had been like a son to her and her husband, and that they had not allowed anyone to touch any of Philip's things.

When Nancy stepped into the garage, she felt relaxed. The thick beige carpet, the pine wood paneling, and the little fireplace that still had a log in it created a cozy atmosphere. The paintings on the walls were magnificent. They looked expensive, and right away Nancy wondered how Philip could ever have afforded such art. There were three of them. The large one that hung over the little fire place showed a wooded area with a river running through it, and in the distance there was a man holding a fishing pole, and next to the man was a brown dog. The silver-framed one that hung over the couch was of an extraordinary blue car that looked alive. It had no wheels, but wings underneath it. The gentle colors and features of the car were inviting. The last picture that Nancy saw was in the little bathroom that had been added onto the garage. This picture was of a young boy standing alone in the center of nothing. A light shone down upon him and lit up his sad brown eyes. It was absolutely compelling. Nancy's first reaction was to hug the child, and her second reaction was to feel frustrated because she couldn't reach him.

Mrs. Portson smiled at Nancy's reactions to the paintings. "They're Philip's paintings. He's gifted. His studio is in our house. There's no room out here for it."

"May I see it?"

Just as Nancy had been surprised by Philip's cozy living quarters and his magnificent talent, she was just as astonished by his studio. Signs of his warm loving nature were in every picture in the room. Mr. Portson came into Philip's workroom and explained some of the pictures to Nancy.

"All these cars," he yelled out, "are cars that no one can drive. Philip was hurt when he couldn't have his driver's license, so he started painting cars. He told me that these cars were the only ones that he could drive, so he painted them from his imagination."

"They're beautiful," Nancy hollered back.

"Yes, and here's his mother."

Nancy looked at the picture that Mr. Portson pointed out. It was of an angel. She was beautiful and made with warm soft colors as most of Philip's paintings were.

"She's imagined too. He never knew his mother," he yelled.

Nancy remembered that Philip had told her on the tape that his mother had died when he was a baby. "This painting, it looks so real. Like she could just fly away from this frame if she wanted to."

"He painted a picture of my wife and me. It's hanging in our bedroom. Looks just like us."

On their way out of the room, Nancy saw a half-finished painting of Philip. Mr. Portson was out of the room when she asked his wife about the painting.

"Oh, that's Philip. He was working on that before he left. I pray to God that they let him go one day, and he gets to come home and finish it. We miss him." She began crying.

Nancy could feel the fragility of Mrs. Portson's thin body while she was lightly hugging her. Her bones were so prominent, and her skin hung loosely onto them. Nancy was afraid she might break something on her if she hugged her too tightly. She loosened up her hold on her. "There, there, Mrs. Portson, everything will be fine." Nancy wondered how she could comfort someone else with lies. How could everything be fine? How could something bad that had already happened be fixed?

Mrs. Portson's voice was shaky. "He's a good boy. He'd never hurt anybody. Ed and I, we've known him for years."

"Philip said that he moved here when he was 18 and that you and your husband were nice people."

"He came to us looking for a place to stay. He said he'd work for us, and he did. When we had some money problems, he went right out and got a job down at the store. He's like a son to us."

They both heard Ed's voice, "the real-estate lady's in the driveway."

"Are you selling your home?"

"Dear, we don't have a choice. Philip's not here to help us out. Ed and I, we can't do the things that we used to. He needs help taking a shower. I need help with housework. We can't mow the lawn, and we can't make repairs on this house."

"There are service companies that can send people out to help you."

"I checked. They don't provide that out here. All they have out here is a nursing home, and Ed and I don't want that. We're going to a retirement apartment in the city if we can sell our home. We'll miss it here, but it hasn't been the same place since Philip left."

"The real-estate lady is here," Ed yelled once more from the bottom of the stairs.

Mrs. Portson walked Nancy to the door. "I want you to stay for dinner."

"Well, I…"

"Please. We seldom have company."

"I have a few more people to visit, but dinner does sound wonderful. Thank you."

Nancy's car was blocked in the driveway by the real-estate woman's truck, and she didn't want to inconvenience her, so she walked down the road to the store. It was a mild day. The breeze and the shade from the trees felt good. She was aware of being alone outside which was not something that could easily happen where she lived. The smell of the country was a nice change for her. The peaceful atmosphere soon had her humming as she walked. Soon, she was singing. It was an over powering feeling of freedom that she was experiencing because there was no one within listening range. In the city, she was restricted to singing in her car.

The long country road seemed to go on forever. It was nearly half of a mile to the store. Nancy prided herself on having obtained natural exercise that seemed healthier than the stationary bicycle in her apartment and the treadmills at the gym.

The door creaked as she opened it. It was a small grocery store, newly painted and very clean, no dust on the shelves. It had new floor tile. Everything looked in order.

"How are you doing Miss?"

Nancy turned to the middle-aged man in the white apron. He had light brown, thin hair, a thick brown mustache, small eyes, and silver framed glasses.

"I'm fine, thank you sir. Are you the store manager?"

"Yes, I'm the owner too. What do you need?"

"I'm writing a book about Jane Fellow's murder."

"Sorry, Miss, but I won't help you with that."

"I'm trying to prove that Philip Securd is innocent."

"He's a good boy."

"I just walked over here from the Portsons' house. They showed me some of his paintings and his apartment. I know he worked for you. He said that you promoted him to Second Assistant Manager."

He laughed. "Yes, well, that made him feel good."

"That was nice of you, Mr.?"

"Barton. Call me Ken."

"My name is Nancy. I wanted to find out how long Philip worked for you and what you thought of him."

"Well, he started working here about. Let's see. I reckon it was about." Ken rubbed his chin. "It was the same year that my father died. So, that would have been six years ago."

"He was a bag boy when he started?"

"Yes, yes, he was. A darn good one too. He was never late to work. Even made it here in a snow storm once." He laughed. "Of course, we didn't have any customers that day. We had two feet of snow. He had to stay the night with my wife and I." He looked at the wall behind himself. "He gave me that painting."

Nancy looked over at the painting on the wall over the cash register. It was a picture of the inside of the store and of Ken working behind the cash register. It was very detailed. Even the cans on the store shelves had labels on them. "Wow, that must have taken him a long time to paint."

"He does everything slow. I don't think that he's always been slow. I don't think he got that way until he got sick."

"What does he have?"

"He say's, he doesn't have anything. That's how he is. He doesn't like to worry anybody, but I know that he's got something wrong with him. He passed out a couple of times when he was working. He'd just get back up and go right back to work like nothing ever happened."

"Do the Portsons know what it is?"

"I don't think they even suspect anything's wrong. Philip doesn't like to worry anybody."

"He said that his doctor told him…" Nancy stopped and decided suddenly to be considerate of Philip's privacy. "Is there a doctor in this town?"

"That'd be Dr. Kebler. I know Philip saw him. I tried to get the doc. to tell me, but he said he couldn't 'cause of confidentiality."

"Where's his office?"

Ken pointed towards the window. "Take that road to the right. Go about two miles down. Then, turn left onto Bisk Road, and it's about half of a mile down from there. His house is beside his office, so if he's closed, just go there. He's usually always home. Ever since his wife left him, he doesn't go anywhere. She used to be a nun but gave it up to marry him. I guess that was a mistake. She certainly can't go back to being a nun. She moved all the way to Minnesota to live with her mother."

"Well, it was nice having met you, Ken. I'd better be heading back. The Portsons invited me to stay for dinner."

"They're such a sweet couple. I sure wish they didn't have to move out. They'll certainly be missed. If only there was a way that Philip could be with them again. That poor boy."

Nancy thought of Philip on her walk back to the Portsons' house. Everyone refers to him as a good boy even though he's 25 years old. He couldn't drive, and he lived out here in the country. His time was spent working in a store, taking care of an elderly couple, painting pictures, and fishing in a river. All this young man wanted in his life was a dog. How did his fingerprints and his DNA wind up in a city alley near a dead woman?

Nancy savored every bite of Mrs. Portson's cooking. It was a meal that Claudia would have killed for: tender, juicy roast beef and smooth mashed potatoes covered in delicious hot gravy, fresh green beans and sweet corn on the cob. It included a colorful salad made with crispy green lettuce and ripe red tomatoes sprinkled with orange shredded cheese and brown square crunchy croutons. The meal ended with warm homemade apple pie that melted in Nancy's mouth.

In her initial short visit, she had come to be treated like family, like a daughter. Mr. and Mrs. Portson hugged and kissed her good-bye, and she hugged and kissed them back. This kind of affection was not something that she was used to with people that she had just met. They invited her back, and she promised to return.

Driving down roads with no streetlights felt weird. The trees that looked so beautiful earlier were scary looking now, like big shadowy monsters. The little grocery store was closed. After traveling two miles, Nancy came to an intersection. She made a left turn onto Bisk Road and traveled about half of a mile before stopping in front of the doctor's office building. The lights were off, so she drove a little farther to the doctor's house.

"Perhaps it's too late." A light was on in the huge brick house, but it was 9:30 p.m. "Oh, stop being silly and go up to the door." Shifting her car into park, "Yes, go." Shifting her car back into drive, "No, don't, it's too late. I shouldn't have stayed at the Portsons' so long. It serves me right. I'll just have to drive all the way out here again tomorrow."

Turning off the headlights, she turned around in his driveway. Quickly, she turned them back on as she headed down the dark road. She turned the volume up on the radio. Music would take her mind off the eerie vibes that she was feeling.

At the end of his road, a large shadowy object darted out from the woods and stopped in front of the car. It happened so quickly that there was no time to brake. Shattering glass, screeching tires, and twisting metal drowned out the music on the radio. As the air bag punched her in the face, Nancy thought about dying. She wondered who would find her body.

When the vehicle quit moving, Nancy realized that she was alive. She touched her head, face, chest, stomach, and felt her legs. Everything seemed to be all right.

After the impact, the car had spun into the woods, smashing the driver's side door up against a huge tree. Trembling, Nancy slid out the passenger side door and walked slowly away from the crushed metal, broken glass, spewing hoses, and hissing air bag. Near by, she found the shadowy object that had caused the crash. It was a deer. It now lay mangled, dead in the road.

Nancy returned to the car and wrenched her keys from the ignition. The tiny flashlight that was once nothing but a decorative ornament on her key chain, now became her only source of light. She stepped over one of the tires that lay in her path. Onward, Nancy moved into the dark with a small dim light that lit up no more than her hand.

Each step she took, for a long time, was in hopes of seeing the doctor's house. By the time she arrived at her destination, she was tired and thirsty. Dr. Kebler's lights went off upstairs as Nancy rang the doorbell.

"Yes," he answered.

Nancy looked at the attractive young man: dark hair, sparkly blue eyes, and prominent jaw. Through his open blue robe, she could see his muscular chest and flat tummy. He had blue pajama bottoms on and matching slippers. She thought that he would be older from what Ken had told her. The feeling was a strange one. Awkwardly, she held out her hand. "Hi, I was in a car accident. I hit a deer."

The doctor reached towards her and took hold of her hand. "Come in. Come in. Here, sit down." He guided her over to a chair in the living room and turned on a light. "Are you hurt?"

"No, I don't think so."

"I'm a doctor," he informed, as he looked her over for injuries.

"Yes, I know."

"You're not from around here?"

"No, I'm not. I was going to visit you earlier, but I decided it was too late. I was planning to visit you tomorrow."

"But you hit a deer on your way home?"

"Right."

"Where's your car at?"

"About half a mile down the road. It's crushed into a tree. The deer wrecked the front of it, and the tree took care of the rest."

"Last year, the mailman hit a deer on my road, and his truck was thrown into the trees. He died instantly. You're lucky."

"Yes, I guess so," Nancy commented though she didn't feel lucky to have a wrecked car and no way home.

"There's a towing service out here, but they're closed right now. Is there some place that you'd like me to drive you?"

"I live quite a long ways from here. I couldn't ask you to do that. Is there a taxi service?"

"They're closed."

"The only people I really know around here are the Portsons. I just met them today. They were telling me about Philip Securd and how he was like a son to them."

"Yes, yes, he was."

"They don't think that he could have murdered Jane Fellow and neither does Ken Barton at the store."

"No, I guess they wouldn't."

Nancy coughed a dry cough.

"Would you like something to drink?"

"Yes, please."

"Brandy will help you relax." He quickly poured her a glass of brandy and himself one too. He sat down in the chair across from her. "So, what did you want to see me about?"

"I'm writing a book about Jane Fellow's murder." She took another drink of her brandy. "I visited Philip in prison. He said that you told him that he didn't have long to live. What does he have?"

"He asked me not to tell anyone. He didn't want the Portsons to worry about him. It wouldn't be ethical for me to tell you."

"He's in prison."

"I know."

"I need to know what he has, or I can't help him."

"You won't be able to help him even if you do know."

"He's mentally slow, and there was no mention of that in the court documents. I don't even think his lawyer had a doctor test him for competency."

"He's competent."

"But he's got something wrong with him, and there was not one document that contained that information in his trial. I don't understand how he could be dying without anyone knowing, not even his lawyer."

"Philip Secürd has an inoperable brain tumor."

"What?"

"I'm surprised that he's still living. It was aggressive."

"What do you mean?"

"It's spreading." He grimaced. "It's malignant."

"Isn't there anything that can be done?"

"No," he barked angrily.

Nancy drew back in her chair. She watched him refill their brandy glasses again. Her eyes searched the walls for a clock. His agitation with her questions alerted her to the idea that he might be overtired.

He took a big gulp of his brandy. "There are some new medicines that have worked on a few patients. His chances would be so slim. Already, it's been two years for him. It's possible that it could be in a dormant stage. That would account for his increased life."

"How is Philip affected by this tumor? What are his symptoms?"

"The destroyed brain cells, the weight of the tumor pressing on critical areas, and the symptoms of distraction all contribute to his inability to process information normally."

"Have you seen any of his paintings?"

"I own one. That's what he used for payment. He painted a portrait of my wife." He looked towards the wall to his right.

"She's beautiful," Nancy commented. There was something odd about the painting, but Nancy couldn't figure out what it was.

"Yes, she is." He looked sad.

Nancy felt uneasy remembering that Ken Barton had told her the doctor's wife had left him. He poured himself more brandy and refilled her glass too.

She felt a bit tipsy as she finished off her third glass of brandy. He started to fill it again, but she covered it with her hand. "No, thank you."

"Would you like for me to drive you over to the Portsons' place? You're welcome to stay here if you like. There's a guestroom upstairs. Your car can be towed in the morning, and no matter how far you live, I want to drive you home tomorrow. I don't mind. Tomorrow's my day off."

"I really hate to ruin your day off."

"You won't. Everyone's always telling me that I need to get out of this house once in a while and away from my office. It would make everyone in town happy if I took you home tomorrow."

"All right then. Thank you."

The grandfather clock in the corner of the room began chiming. Nancy counted eleven chimes. "Shall I drive you over to the Portsons' house?" He waited for her response. When there wasn't one, he added, "or shall I show you to the guestroom?"

"I think it's too late to be waking up the Portsons."

He smiled. "Follow me to the guestroom."

She followed him up the oak wood staircase with the glittering chandelier that hung over the center of the room. The whole house was decorated beautifully. Nancy wondered when she would be able to afford such nice things and a gorgeous home. The whole house was immaculate. For his wife being away, he was doing a wonderful job at cleaning, or maybe he had a maid. Of course, that was it, he had a maid. A doctor would be far too busy to keep his house this spotless. The guestroom had a door that led outside to a balcony.

The doctor told her to make herself comfortable, and then he disappeared down the hallway. Nancy closed the door and pulled back the fluffy flowered bedspread revealing clean white sheets.

There was a tap at the door. "Nancy."

She opened the door. The doctor handed her a white silky nightgown. "My wife is out of town visiting her mother. I don't think that she would mind if you borrowed this for the night."

She accepted the gown and thanked him once again for his hospitality. They once again wished each other a good night, and he left. Nancy dressed and got into bed. She snuggled up against the soft pillow and realized how unpredictable her life was. She thought, who would have ever guessed that I would be spending tonight in a stranger's house and sleeping in his wife's nightgown?

CHAPTER 9

▼

MEDICAL REPORTS

Nancy woke up at nine o'clock. She dressed and ran downstairs. On the table in the dining room, she saw her purse covered in a light layer of dirt. Beside it, was a note: "I removed your purse from your car, and I phoned the towing service for you. Your car is at the Denten Towing Yard. I had an emergency. I'll be back soon. Keith Kebler."

While Nancy was waiting in the living room for Dr. Kebler to return, she noted the hard wood floors and how shinny they were; she could see her reflection. She examined the grandfather clock and some antiques. All of the books on his shelves were about medicines, surgeries, and diseases.

The doctor stepped into the house through the back door. Nancy jumped, startled. "Oh, you scared me."

"Sorry. I didn't mean to. Would you like to go to breakfast?"

"Yes, thank you for getting my purse and having my car towed." She glanced at his phone. "Would it be all right if I make a call to my insurance company?"

With the doctor's permission, Nancy phoned the claims department and made the necessary arrangements to get her car inspected by an adjuster.

"I'm sorry, I had to leave. Brian Robbin dropped a pickle jar on his foot, and his toe needed a few stitches."

"I heard that name Robbin before, but I can't remember from who."

"The Robbins live down the road a ways from the Portsons."

"I still can't remember who mentioned them." She thought for a few moments. "I know, it was Philip. He said that they were going to give him a dog."

"Did he?" The Doctor commented looking upset. "Are you ready to go?"

"Dr. Kebler…"

"Keith."

"Keith, would you please give me Philip's medical records so that I can confirm that he has a brain tumor? I might be able to get him into a hospital and out of the prison for a while. He's terribly unhappy, and he looks sick."

He looked at her and took a moment to think about it. "I understand that you want to do what's best for Philip, but it just wouldn't be ethical for me to give you his records."

"Would it be ethical for him to die in prison without receiving the medical attention that he needs?"

"There is nothing that can save him. Medical treatments would only prolong his suffering. Is that ethical?"

"He deserves a chance to live."

Dr. Kebler shook his head in dismay. "I'll be right back." He went up the stairs and returned in a few moments with a folder in his hands. He opened it and showed her the paperwork on Philip's brain tumor. "This is malignant. See here on this CAT scan report how the tumor's spreading. The affected area is growing. It's very progressive."

Nancy wondered why Philip's medical records were upstairs in the doctor's house and not in his office. She looked at the paper-work as he showed it to her, one report after the other, and she made mental notes about what was important. It only took that sweet second when he stepped away from her to answer his phone that allowed her the time to take what she needed.

As he returned the folder back up stairs, Nancy hugged her purse to her hoping that he would not check for anything missing in that folder. He returned smiling. "Now, that you understand Philip's sit-uation, shall we go to breakfast?"

"That'll be great." She smiled to his face, and when he turned his back to get his keys, she sighed with relief.

The first thing that Dr. Kebler did when they got into his car was to turn on his phone and listen to his messages. "I don't mean to be rude, but I must phone some of these people back. Most of them are my patients," he explained. After several lengthy phone conversa-tions, he put his phone away.

Breakfast went quicker than Nancy thought it would. He drove past the one restaurant in town and didn't stop until they reached the city. Then, he swung the car into the drive-thru at the first fast food restaurant. They ate their ham and cheese bagels and drank their orange juices in route to Nancy's apartment.

Nancy was disappointed that neither the trip nor the breakfast allowed for time to discuss Philip. When they arrived at her apart-ment, she pleaded with him to come inside for a cup of coffee.

Dr. Kebler sat rigidly on the couch. "Thank you for the coffee." He gulped it quickly.

Nancy wondered how he could drink his coffee without sipping it. She knew it was steaming hot. "Philip's art amazes me," she started off.

He nodded his head, and set his empty mug down on the coffee table in front of him. "Phil aah aah choo. Aah aah choo."

"Bless you."

Clansy jumped up on the couch, and the doctor sneezed uncontrollably. "I'm allergic to cats," he explained as he made his way quickly towards the door.

"I'll put him in another room. Please stay."

"I'm sorry. Aah choo. It won't help. Aah choo. Thank you for the coffee." He pulled his handkerchief from his pocket and covered his nose.

Nancy followed him to the door. "Thank you for bringing me home and letting me stay the night."

Claudia was entering Nancy's apartment as Dr. Kebler was leaving. "Oh, you have company." She smiled.

Nancy spoke quickly. "Claudia this is Dr. Keith Kebler and Dr. Kebler this is Claudia, my friend."

"Nice to meet you. Ah-choo. Good-bye."

Claudia followed after him to see what he was driving. She entered Nancy's apartment smiling. "And, I thought you worked like a dog on your weekends."

"I do."

"Dating a doctor who drives a Mercedes?"

"No, of course, not. It was work related."

"Work related?"

"Yes, I was researching Philip Secured's story and everything checks out."

"Was that his doctor?"

"Yes."

"Did you check him out?" She laughed.

"Knock it off."

"Why was he here?"

"I spent the night at his house."

"Checked him out thoroughly I see."

"It wasn't like that. A deer ran in front of my car, and my car's a piece of metal junk right now in a towing yard in Denten. He simply let me stay at his house for the night."

"He's good looking."

"Claudia, I was in a car accident. Aren't you even going to ask me if I'm all right?"

"Are you all right? You look all right."

"I'm all right."

"So what's the doctor like?"

"He's allergic to cats."

"So, he's out?"

"Yes."

"Silly, you get rid of the cat, not the man."

"He's not my man. He's married."

"What's his wife like?"

"I don't know. She wasn't there." She answered Claudia's raised eyebrows. "They're separated."

"That's promising."

"Claudia, that's enough."

"How did your date with Jimmy turn out?"

"I don't know. I'm still in denial. What's happening with our strike?"

"Not a damn thing. No one's talking." She plopped down on the couch. "No one's giving in. I'm thinking about becoming the owner of the little paper here in our city."

"*News To Know?*"

"Yes, word is, it's for sale. Jimmy said that he might invest in it. He received a large sum of money from a relative of his, and he doesn't know what to do with it. Isn't that a shame? Money always winds up in the wrong person's hands. Wouldn't you like to date him again?"

"You want his money; you date him."

"He's not interested in me or I would. What's for lunch?"

"I'll order you some Greek food, and then I'm going to tell you all about Philip Secured and what a wonderful person he is."

"You're not going to rot my teeth out are you?"

"What are you talking about?"

"Nancy, I'm worried about you. I'm afraid that you're trying to put a halo on a murderer."

"Give me a break, Claudia. I'm not sugarcoating anything this time. This guy is nothing like the newspapers, the court, or Richard Fellow portrayed him to be."

"Wait a second. Are you forgetting something here? We write the stories in those papers. We didn't portray him to be anything. We merely covered the story, and that's our job."

"Claudia, we do portray people to be what fits the story sometimes. We never interviewed him. No one did. We ate what was fed to us, and the whole thing was written up one sided, the prosecution's side of it. Philip's defense attorney didn't have a weak case. He deliberately didn't do his job to defend him."

"Calm down. We may have made a mistake. Maybe he's not who we thought he was. Go ahead; tell me what you found out."

CHAPTER 10

▼

THREAT

Nancy had taken the medical reports about Philip's condition to the prison, and she pushed for the warden to send Philip to the hospital for treatment. For three weeks, he had been hospitalized, and for three weekends in a row, Nancy visited him. She had also been visiting the Portsons regularly.

Nancy finished drinking her coffee. She carried the cup to the sink. Mrs. Portson offered her some more.

"No, thank you. I better head home. I want to give Philip this letter today. He loves you both so much, and these letters really help him feel better."

"Is he going to be in the hospital long?" Mr. Portson asked.

"I think he is."

Nancy had stepped outside onto the front porch. Mrs. Portson followed her. Nancy knew that she wouldn't be able to avoid what was coming. She turned to look at her and could see the concern in her eyes before she even asked, "What's wrong with him?"

"I'm not sure, but I know that your letters help him feel better," she answered sympathetically.

"I wish that we could go and see him."

"I wish that you could too. If my friend wasn't helping me, I wouldn't be able to see him either."

Nancy saw Mrs. Portson reach out to hug her as she usually did before she left. Just as Nancy moved towards her, Mrs. Portson yelled out, "Oh, dear, look! Your car!"

"My car?" Nancy with her arms still held out, turned and looked where Mrs. Portson's eyes were staring. "My tires!"

All four tires on the little white rental car were flat. Nancy walked around the car to examine it for anymore damage, and that is when she saw the writing. In black bold lettering that went from the bottom of the side window to the bottom of the door were the words: **FIRST WARNING**. There were scrape marks on the front of the hood. It had been pried open. Nancy lifted the hood. Someone had poured a sticky brown substance over the engine. The dipstick from the oil was missing along with the cap to the radiator. Both of the compartments were filled with the syrupy liquid.

Mrs. Portson looked scared. "I'll call the sheriff, dear."

When Sheriff Clifford arrived, he and Nancy examined the car. He shook his head. "Well, it looks like vandalism all right. I've been the sheriff in this town for twenty years, and we never had a vandalism report like this one. Actually, we don't get many reports about vandalism. This will be my first one to write in ages. You have any idea who might have done this? Is there anyone at all that you suspect?"

"No."

"Your name sounds familiar. Are you the lady who's been asking all the questions about Philip Securd?"

Nancy nodded her head.

"You also ran into a deer out by the Doc's place?"

"Yes."

"That car was smashed up pretty good. I seen it being towed through town about three or four weeks ago. It didn't look like it could be fixed."

"It couldn't. That's why I'm driving this rented car. What am I going to do about the car?"

"Call your insurance company. That's what insurance is for."

"Yeah, right. That car rental company is going to go nuts over this. I had to wait hours before they would give me this puddle jumper. They probably won't have another car to give me. Is there a place around here that rents cars?"

"No, and it's Joe's day off. This is his fishing day. He never gives up his fishing day to drive anybody anywhere."

Answering the perplexed expression on her face, he said, "He's the taxi cab driver."

"It will take hours before that company brings me another car if they bring me one at all," she complained.

"Don't get yourself all upset over this. Life's too short to have a hot temper when something goes wrong. What you could do is take in a movie, a nice lunch in town. Have someone show you around this place. Maybe, spend some time down at the river. It's beautiful this time of year."

Nancy raised her eyebrows and then knitted them together as she shook her head. "I don't think I want to see anymore of this town. Look at my car."

"Whoever did this appears to be trying to tell you something. It might have something to do with all the questions about Philip Secured that you've been asking people."

"What do you mean?"

"Well, this is a small town. People knew Philip, and maybe they're afraid that you mean him harm."

"I'm trying to help Philip. I've told everyone that."

"Other people have said that too, and they didn't help him one bit. It makes it hard to trust strangers when they say one thing and do another. If you change your mind about seeing the place, let me know."

"I thought this was a one sheriff town."

"I have a deputy. Besides, there's not enough crime around here to keep us both busy all day. Don't worry, I'll keep a look out for the person who did this. Like I said, it's probably just somebody trying to protect Philip. You needn't take that warning seriously." He leaned down a bit to look her in the face. "There's a good movie starting in a short while that I'd enjoy taking you to." The Sheriff wiped his right hand firmly across his forehead patting down his thick blond hair.

His small, dull blue eyes looked into her eyes, and he smiled, opening his thick lips to reveal a straight even row of big white teeth.

Nancy watched him lick his lips slowly. She took a step back. "Thank you for the offer, but I feel terrible about the car. I think I'd be better off spending some time with the Portsons. Thank you anyway."

After Nancy phoned the rental car place and learned that they would not give her another car, she phoned Claudia and left a message on her answering machine. Then, she sat outside on the porch to wait.

The day was lovely, and she knew that the sheriff was right: there was no use in getting upset. The fresh summer air, the woodsy green countryside, and the birds singing made it difficult for her to remain angry.

Mrs. Portson walked out onto the porch. "Lovely day isn't it, dear?"

"Yes, yes, it is. I think I will go for a walk down to the river. Would you like to join me?"

"No, thank you, dear. I'm glad you're feeling better. Head out that way," she said pointing down the road. "You'll come to the water in a little while, dear."

Nancy knew that she would be walking for about a mile. She started out at a brisk pace. Her emotional anger dissipated as her physical energy increased. The soft warm breeze felt good on her back, neck, and shoulders like a caressing massage. It was not long before she was out of the sight of Mrs. Portson. Once again, as it did that day when she had walked to the store, it struck her that she was alone. And like before, she was overcome with a feeling of peaceful joy. The urge to sing overtook her. It wasn't long before she was humming and then singing. Before she sang that last word, she saw the doctor suddenly walking up beside her.

"Sounds like you're in a pretty good mood," he said.

Startled, she stopped walking. "Where did you come from?"

"The path in the woods. I was doing some fishing."

She saw that he was carrying a small black leather case and nothing more.

"Where are you headed?" he asked.

"To the river," she answered wondering where his fishing pole was.

"I'll show you a shortcut. Follow me."

She followed him through the woods. "Someone vandalized my rental car."

"Why would someone do that?"

"I don't know."

The path was worn. It didn't take long for them to reach the river. "This is beautiful. Looks crystal clear. I can see the bottom." She smiled at the doctor, but he did not return the smile. She studied his reflection in the water. He was handsome. That was the same thing that she had thought about him when she had first met him.

He bent down and picked up a huge rock. "Someone called me yesterday, a lawyer. He said that you gave him my number. He questioned me about Philip's brain tumor." The doctor plunged the rock into the water. The ripples broke up the reflection.

Nancy made eye contact with him. "If it was Attorney Stenson, I did give him your number. He's investigating Philip's trial. He thinks that he might be able to help him by proving that he didn't receive a fair trial. I'm not sure what he can do to help, but I knew that Philip's medical history would help him."

"I know that you took those medical reports, and I want them back."

"I gave them to the University Hospital near the prison after I showed them to Attorney Stenson."

"You stole those."

"The hospital director said that the cancer team needed them. Philip's receiving help now. He's been in the hospital for three weeks now, and they're trying a new medicine on him. It's been known to cure a few other patients. Its success rate is not that high overall, but for the few that it helps, it shrinks their tumors down to nothing."

She studied his face. He averted his eyes from hers. His lips were pursed.

"Aren't you glad that Philip is being helped?"

"Yes," he answered gruffly. "But what good is a lawyer going to do for him? Are you hoping to get Philip into a mental institution?"

"Dr. Kebler, I…"

"Keith," he reminded her.

"Keith, I don't think Philip did it. I'm not trying to get him into a mental institution. I'm trying to set him free. I think that he was framed."

"If he was, who do you think framed him?"

"I don't know. I just know that he couldn't have done it."

"That's quite an allegation that you're making. That might make someone nervous."

"Who?"

"The person who framed him perhaps?"

The murderer, Nancy thought. He's right.

He stared into her big brown eyes. "I'm wondering who would have done all that damage to your car?"

His peering blue eyes glared at her making him look sinister. "I...I...I don't know," she stammered.

Nancy took a noticeable step backwards away from him. He smiled. She nervously smiled back. "I'm only trying to help Philip."

"I'd be careful if I were you."

She heard herself letting out a heavy sigh as she watched him walk away. It was too difficult for her to shake off his strange words of advice. The only safe thing to do now was to run back to the Portsons' house. After scanning the woods on all sides, Nancy ran to the path. Someone's watching me, she thought. She alternated running and walking. No matter that her eyes saw no one, she felt someone was following her. "Thank God," she whispered when she saw the sheriff's car coming down the dirt road.

He pulled up along side her. "Were you at the river?"

"Yes, it's nice."

"Feel better now?"

"I'm not angry anymore about my car." Nancy waited for him to speak hoping that he would invite her to the movies again.

"Well, I'll see you around."

He started to drive off. "Wait," she called out. She jogged a few steps towards his car. "I was thinking that it would be nice to see a movie."

"Would you like to come with me to the movie house?"

"Yes, I would, thank you."

"Hop in." He smiled at her. "I know a great place for lunch. It's the only restaurant in town, but don't worry, the food's tasty."

Nancy recognized the restaurant. It was the same one that Dr. Kebler had driven by the day he had driven her home. The décor wasn't much to look at, but the food was delicious.

The movie house was a huge farmhouse that had been converted into a movie theater. Sheriff Clifford explained to Nancy that the town did not have enough tax dollars to pay for a decent renovation; therefore, the theater was actually a house. The movie house supplied popcorn, lemonade, and a movie for one dollar. The dollar was spent purchasing new DVDs for the DVD machine, so that they would have a selection of movies to watch on the 61" screen.

The Sheriff and Nancy took their seats beside three people who were already waiting for the movie to begin. The three people said hello to the sheriff and to Nancy. To her surprise, they knew her name. Two of them said that they had heard about who she was from the Portsons, and the other one said that she had heard about her from Ken Barton.

When the sheriff dropped her back off at the Portsons' house, she phoned Claudia and was about to leave another message, but Claudia answered. Nancy paced back and forth as far as the telephone cord would allow her to go in the Portsons' kitchen. "Claudia, you've got to come and get me. Because, the car rental company won't give me another car, that's why. It was towed to Pete's Garage. Why all the questions? The insurance company is paying, the one through the car rental place, and they're sending someone out to pick it up. I did try, but they won't give me another one. No, I don't let people walk all over me. Claudia, are you coming or not?"

Nancy hung up the phone and smiled at the Portsons. "She's coming. Claudia's my best friend. Really, she is."

Claudia arrived in time to have dinner. She left the Portsons' house with a bag of Mrs. Portson's delicious green fried tomatoes and other goodies. "She can cook. I'd love it if she were my mother. I was raised on fast food. Maybe they can adopt me. Is it legal to have two sets of parents?"

Nancy buckled up her seat belt. "I met them first, so if it is legal, they're mine."

Claudia started driving. "So, are you going to tell me about this sheriff that you've been seeing, or must I rely on the gossip?"

"Who told you that I was seeing the sheriff?"

"The guy at that little store. I had to stop for directions. He told me that you went out on a date with the sheriff today. Lunch and a movie ring a bell?"

"Yes, but it wasn't a date."

"What was it then?"

"It was fear. I wouldn't have gone if it wasn't for the doctor."

Nancy told Claudia about what Dr. Kebler had said to her when she was at the river. She also explained that he had gone fishing without a fishing pole.

"Do you think the doctor framed Philip?"

"It's possible, Claudia. He could have easily gotten a hold of some of Philip's blood. But it still doesn't make any sense. I mean, why would he want to hurt Philip? What could Philip have possibly done to him? There's no motive."

"Nancy, what I don't understand is how Philip painted those pictures at the Portsons'. If he's as mentally challenged as you say that he is, then how did he paint those pictures?"

"I don't know. Take the road on the right up ahead."

"Are you sure that he painted them?"

"Yes. Every one in town seems to know about his talent. The doctor, the storeowner, and the Portsons all have paintings by Philip."

"Nancy, I have to tell you something about Richard."

"He's not back from his trip yet, is he?"

"No."

"Good, because if he knew how far I was on his book, he'd probably go nuts."

"How far are you?"

"Not even started."

"Why not?"

"I've been busy investigating everything."

"Well, remember when he resigned from being mayor?"

"After his wife was murdered."

"Do you remember that he was planning to run for governor?"

"Yes."

"He's still going to."

"Really. Well, I think that's great. It shows tremendous courage. He has had to deal with the terrible tragedy of his wife's murder. Honestly, I give him a lot of credit."

"Remember when I told you that I was trying to become the owner of *News To Know*?"

"You said that you were thinking about it." Nancy grabbed onto the handle on the roof. "Claudia, slow down."

"I can't."

"Try using the brake."

"No, what I mean is that I can't afford to do it. It's too expensive."

"Well, it's a lame paper anyway. You'd be better off sinking your energy elsewhere."

"They already have web presses and a circulation."

"Only pet owners buy *News To Know*."

"I'm going to turn that paper around."

"With what? You just said that you couldn't afford to become the owner."

"Alone I can't, but I'm going to have two silent partners: Jimmy and Richard."

"Fellow?"

"Yes. I promised him lots of publicity. Richard will need all the attention that he can get. When I told him that I could turn that little paper around, he offered to invest in me. The timing was perfect. He and Jimmy are my backers, and guess who I'm hiring first?"

"How did you get Jimmy to invest in you?"

"I told him that Richard was backing me, and I guess Jimmy thought it was a smart thing to do. I told you that he didn't know what to do with that inheritance money."

"Is he really a silent partner?"

"I hope he stays silent. Now, let me get to my point here. I'm hiring you to write for my newspaper."

"I can't."

"Don't worry. Jimmy won't be working in the same office as you. I promise."

"It's not that, Claudia. I can't because I don't have the time."

Claudia hit the brakes. Her eyes locked with Nancy's.

"After I get this thing wrapped up. Claudia, will you please drive? I'll work for you as soon as I'm finished with Richard's book."

"I guess I better tell you the truth."

Nancy looked at Claudia puzzled.

"Richard's on his way back."

"Claudia!"

"I didn't want you to get upset."

"He's not coming to my place, is he?"

"Nancy, he told me that he doesn't want you to work on the book anymore. He said that he would tell you himself, but I thought I should tell you."

"What?"

"He said that he needs to put all of his effort and his friends' efforts into his campaign. He doesn't have much time to try and gain voters."

"But what about that big advance he took from that publisher?"

"I don't know, Nancy. I didn't ask him, and that's not our problem."

"I can't leave Philip hanging. Claudia, I'm not stopping. If Richard doesn't want me to write his book, fine, but I'm still going to help Philip. I've got to."

When Claudia pulled into Nancy's parking space at her apartment, they both spotted Richard's Mark VIII parked near the entrance.

"Claudia! You said that he was on his way back."

"He was. People aren't traveling by horse drawn carriages anymore."

Nancy stepped out of the car and waited for Claudia. "Well, aren't you getting out?"

"No, I have something that I have to do. I'm running a business now. I have to start hiring a staff."

"Claudia, I don't want to talk to Richard by myself."

"Quit being a baby and get in there. He's probably waiting on your doorstep. I told him that I'd have you back home around this time, but I honestly didn't know that he was going to be waiting for you."

Richard Fellow was leaning up against the wall in the hallway. He was talking on his cellular phone, and he didn't see Nancy. She moved towards her apartment but stopped short when she heard him say, "no, don't hurt her. You don't have to. I'm at her place right now. Right, I'll take care of her. She'll stop. She's a friend of mine, and I don't want her hurt. I told you, I'd take care of it, and I am. Look, I have to go. She should be here any minute."

Nancy backed out down the hallway and hid around the corner. She waited for a minute and then made herself cough as she entered into his view. "Oh, Richard." She acted surprised. "Claudia said that you wanted to see me."

He moved quickly towards her and gave her a hug. "Did Claudia tell you what I wanted to see you about?"

"No, but she did say that you were running for governor. I think that's terrific, Richard. You were a wonderful mayor. You'll do our state proud."

She invited him into her apartment and fixed them both some ice tea. He relaxed on the couch and petted Clansy. "Nancy, I'm not going to do the book. I've decided against it."

"But, Richard, you already paid me an advance, and you received an advance."

"Nancy, Nancy, Nancy, let me worry about that."

"Richard, it's so much more than just a book. It's someone's life. I think Philip was framed."

He shot up from the couch. "Nancy, I don't want to hear this. I'm telling you to quit. I hired you, and now I'm telling you to quit."

"Richard, don't you want the right person in prison? The real killer is out there running free. Walking around! He may even kill again. Richard, we have to stop him, and the only way to do that is to prove that we have the wrong man. Philip didn't do it."

"Nancy, stop it. I went to court. He did it. That bastard murdered my wife. You better understand that." He realized that he was shouting at her. "I'm sorry, Nancy." He sat back down on the couch.

She saw his eyes begin to water. "Richard," she said softly. "I have a shirt that one of the witnesses gave me, and it has your wife's blood on it. That autopsy was wrong. She couldn't have died before 9:00 p.m., because at that time, she was still alive. She was at a party store trying to get away from a man in a jogging suit. He dragged her into his truck and…"

"Nancy, how do you know that it's her blood on that shirt?"

"I sent it to a crime lab through a friend of mine. It matched your wife's DNA Richard."

"Where's this shirt at?"

"It's…I think in my…Let me go look for it. I'll be right back." She was right back but not with the shirt. "Sorry, I couldn't find it. I know that I didn't give the shirt or the DNA report to Attorney Stenson yet. The DNA report took quite a bit of time. I had dropped it off at the lab right after I bought it from Mr. Nec."

"Who's he?"

"The witness that saw your wife at the party store that night. If the police would have believed him, your wife might not have been murdered."

"Who's this attorney you're talking about?"

"He's Philip's attorney. Did you know that Philip was mentally slow and has a fatal brain tumor?"

He turned pale and looked dazed. "No, no, I didn't know."

"I think he was framed Richard. That shirt will prove that Philip couldn't have murdered your wife at the time that Josephine Wilderk said that she saw him murdering her. Richard, this new evidence will reopen Philip's case. There will be a new trial."

"No, Nancy there won't be. I don't need this. I'm running for governor. That case is over and done. I'm not going through all of that again and neither is my family. I have two children to think about."

"Richard, there's an innocent man in prison."

"Nancy, that's not true."

"Richard, what if I can prove that it is?"

"Nancy, what if you're wrong? Think about it, Nancy. It's been a year, and no more women have been murdered. Remember what the criminologist said. He said that it looked like the work of a serial killer."

"There was only one murder, Richard."

"We stopped him."

"Who stopped him?"

He shook his head. "Nancy, he did it. The slashes, they were, they were…" He began crying. She hugged him and held him until he finished.

After using her bathroom, he drank a glass of water and returned to the couch. Running his fingers roughly through his hair, he said, "I know that we did the right thing, Nancy. We knew he did it. I know that you don't understand, but we did the right thing."

"Who's we? What did you do?"

"Nancy, what about my wife? Doesn't she deserve some of your sympathy? Why so much sympathy for him? Why?" He stopped yelling. "Nancy, if you care at all about innocent victims, you'll give that shirt and that DNA report to the Chief of Police, Ted Randall."

Nancy was shaking by the time that he left. She wondered what and whom he was talking about. What was the right thing that they did? Who were they? Why did Richard want her to give the shirt and the DNA report to the Chief of Police? Chief Randall, she knew had led the investigation of Jane's murder. Was he one of the people that Richard was talking about? What did he do? While Nancy had plenty of unanswered questions, she was positive about one thing: she was not giving that shirt or that DNA report to Richard or Chief Randall.

CHAPTER 11

▼

EVIDENCE

The next morning, Nancy woke up on the couch. She was surprised that she had been that tired. She remembered phoning Sister Roletta for a ride to the hospital last night. Then, she thought about the whereabouts of that DNA report and Mr. Nec's shirt until she thought herself to sleep.

As long as Nancy pretended to be Sister Roletta's assistant, she was allowed to visit Philip at the hospital. When the nun pulled into the parking lot, Nancy was dressed in the habit that Sister Roletta had loaned her three weeks ago.

Philip's hospital room was small with a tiny bathroom to the right of it. The walls in his room were white and so bright that they gave Nancy a headache. Philip was wearing a blue hospital gown, and he had an IV of morphine feeding into his arm. He smiled and pulled himself up into a sitting position on his bed. "Hello."

"Hi, Philip. I brought you a letter from the Portsons."

"Oh, thanks." He tried to open it, but he was too weak.

"Here, let me get that for you." Nancy took it and opened it. She held onto it for a second remembering that he had asked her to read him his first letter from the Portsons. That had been during his first couple of weeks in the hospital. Now, that he was settled in, she thought maybe he would prefer to read this letter to himself and enjoy some privacy.

"Will you please read it?" he asked.

"Are you sure?"

"I can't read."

"Why not?"

"I tried, but I can't read."

Nancy thought about that for a second. Something seemed untrue about his statement. Then, she realized what it was. "But Philip, you worked for Ken Barton at the store."

"I never had to read anything."

"How did you take inventory?"

"I can count how many of something there is."

Nancy realized that Philip was right, a person could count how much celery there was and potatoes and...but, what about soup labels? Yes, they could even count the different colored labels, the ones that had a picture of chicken soup, or the ones that had a picture of beef soup.

She concluded that he could not write either. "That's why you haven't written the Portsons any letters since you've been in prison?"

"I can write with pictures, but no one gave me any paper or anything to draw with."

Nancy ran right down to the gift shop and bought Philip a pad of drawing paper, a set of colored markers, and a drawing pencil. Her shopping bag was inspected by the elderly white man who was the security guard on duty. He pulled out the markers and read the description, nontoxic. Satisfied, he placed them back into the bag. He pulled out the large fat round pencil. "He can't have this."

"What?"

"It's sharp."

"It's soft lead. Look at it. It doesn't even need a pencil sharpener. You just peel off the outside cover when it gets low. It can't get any sharper than that."

He dropped it back into the bag. He pulled out the large envelope and the package of stamps and dropped them back into the bag.

Nancy printed the Portsons' address on the large envelope for Philip. "This should do it. When your pictures are finished, just place them in this envelope and put the stamps on it and the Portsons will receive it."

Philip gave her a weak smile. He drew slowly, complaining that he used to be faster at it. Nancy knew it was the medicine and the radiation treatments that were causing his fatigue.

"Don't worry Philip. You'll get better."

Sister Roletta stepped in. "I'm finished with my rounds."

"Take care Philip. I'll try to visit you again."

"Okay, Sister. I'm ready to go." Nancy was thankful to have been a writer and editor on the newspaper. She had met Sister Roletta when she covered the story about the church vandalism. By publicizing the vandalism, Nancy was able to help the church receive enough donations to repair the church doors and to replace the broken items.

Sister Roletta dropped Nancy off at her apartment. There were two police cars in front of the building.

"What is going on I wonder," Sister Roletta commented.

Nancy stepped out of the car and stood beside it. "Oh, it's probably the Henkersons again. They're a young couple who live next door to me. All they do is fight." She pulled off the habit revealing her shorts and shirt.

The nun shook her head sadly. She pulled a business card from her glove box and handed it to Nancy. "Please, tell your neighbors to come to the church for free marriage counseling."

Nancy folded the habit the best she could and handed it to Sister Roletta through the car window, and she placed the nun's business card into the pocket of her shorts. "I'll do that. Thank you." She waved good-bye as the nun drove away. Then, she ran into the building and towards her apartment.

Clansy was in the hallway meowing. "What are you doing out here?" Nancy's eyebrows knitted together as she tried to figure out how her pet got loose. She knelt down and her cat leaped into her arms. Holding Clansy to her chest, nervously petting his head, she walked around the corner of the hallway. There, at the doorway to her apartment, was a crowd of tenants, including the Henkersons. All of them were staring into her apartment. The door was dangling from its broken hinges, and six police officers were literally tearing her place apart.

"What are you doing?" she hollered out.

"We have a search warrant."

"Why?"

"We're not inclined to say, but it involves narcotics."

It was hours before the police officers finally left. Nancy was moving from room to room trying to put her things back in place when Claudia rushed into the apartment.

"What the hell happened in here?"

"I told you, they tore my place apart." Nancy bent down, picked up her green throw pillow off the floor, and then stared at the bare couch.

"I know what you said on the phone, but this, this is awful. It looks like a rock band had a hotel party or something in here. How disgusting! And they wonder why people call them pigs."

"That's not the half of it." Her eyes watered.

"Oh, don't cry, Nancy."

"Look at my couch. Where are my cushions?"

Claudia climbed over the toppled furniture and the scattered items and made her way into Nancy's spare bedroom. "I think I found one."

Nancy had tears streaking her cheeks. "They tore up my scrapbook."

Claudia followed her gaze over to the broken shelves and to the pages of her scrapbook that were scattered near and around the other books on the floor. "When you called me, you were so panicky; I couldn't really understand you too well. I had no idea that it was this bad. If I'd known, I would have come sooner."

"Where did you go after I called you?"

"To visit my boyfriend."

"The police officer that arrested Jimmy?"

"Yes."

"Did you tell him what happened to my apartment?"

"Yes. He said that it's rare that they get the wrong apartment, but it sometimes happens. Did the Chief of Police apologize to you?"

"Oh, yes. He came over and apologized in person, that big buffoon."

"What did he say?"

"He said that he was sorry that his narcotics department is run by incompetent young officers who can't read addresses. It was all a big mistake. Who's going to tell my neighbors that, Claudia? They must think that I've done something horribly wrong to be treated like this. All a big mistake!"

"You should sue them."

"I was thinking of something far worse than that."

"Killing them wouldn't help."

"Do you want to help me ransack the Chief's home?"

"Sue them for everything that they broke and for your cleaning time. This is going to take a lot of time."

"Claudia, the time!" She looked at her watch. "I have a meeting with Attorney Stenson."

"You better call and cancel."

"I promised to meet Attorney Stenson about Philip and those blood stains on Mr. Nec's shirt. He wants me to bring him the shirt. He said with that and those DNA results, Philip's new trial is as good as done. I just have to get that evidence to him, but I don't remember what I did with the shirt or the DNA report."

"Retrace your steps from the time you picked them up from the crime lab."

"I don't know, Claudia. I can't think."

"Let's go out on your balcony. Maybe some fresh air will help."

Claudia picked up the knocked over chair on the balcony and set it next to the other one by the table. She watched Nancy straighten her ivy plant and repack the dirt around it. "They should be straightening this place back up, not us. Sit down, Nancy, and try to think about what you did with that shirt and that report."

Nancy sat down. "I know that I picked them up."

"When?"

"It was last week sometime. I wanted to put them someplace where they'd be secure until I needed them. Oh, I know. I locked them in the trunk of the rental car. That's where they are. I know because I was going to visit Philip yesterday, right after I left the Portsons' house, and afterwards, I was thinking of giving the evidence to his attorney because Stenson's office isn't far away from the hospital. The shirt and the report are in the trunk of that rental car out in Denten unless the company picked up the car today like they said they were going to."

Claudia smiled with excitement. "Let me get them for you. You relax."

"I can't relax here."

"Well, you can't leave. The door's broke. Someone could come in and steal your stuff. You better stay here. I'll just ask the manager at that car rental place to show me the car, and I'll get the stuff out of the trunk. No problem."

"It might not even be at that company. It might still be sitting at Pete's garage in Denten."

"Well, if it's not at the company, I'll drive out to Denten."

"Pete's garage won't be open this late."

"I'll go tomorrow morning then. Now, don't worry, I'll get the shirt and the report and everything will be fine."

"Thank you, Claudia. You're my best friend. I don't know what I'd do without you."

Claudia left, and Clansy followed after her. Nancy chased after her cat, scooping him up just as Claudia reached the passenger door of Richard Fellow's Mark VIII. Nancy watched Claudia get into Richard's car and slam the door shut. Quickly, she moved away from the glass front doors of the apartment building, and then she slowly angled her head so that she could peek out the doors without being seen. The tires squealed as the car sped away.

Nancy ran, cradling her cat, back to her apartment. Immediately, she phoned Attorney Jack Stenson and told him to hurry over to her place. She told him only that it was urgent.

Nancy straightened some of her things up while she waited for him. She thought about how to secure her apartment from thieves and settled on the idea of pushing her couch up against the broken door and leaving by way of the fire escape attached to the balcony.

Jack Stenson pulled into the parking lot in his black Corvette. He looked almost like a live Ken doll: short blonde hair, blue eyes, tanned skin, and the facial features of a male model. The extra thing that he had that Ken dolls didn't, besides genitalia, was a potbelly. Jack was about to exit his car, but spotted Nancy running towards him. She had been sitting on a bench near the parking lot. "What's going on?" he asked after reading the anxious look on her face.

"I appreciate this, really, I do," she said while climbing into the passenger side of his car. "We need to hurry. Claudia is helping Richard, and she is going after that DNA report and Mr. Nec's shirt. I need you to drive me to Denten so that we can save Philip. We have to beat Claudia to that car."

"What car? And, why did you hang up on me?"

"The police might be tapping my phone and bugging my apartment."

He laughed. "Yeah, right." Jack looked at her expecting her to laugh. Seeing her tense facial expression, he became concerned. "You're serious."

"Jack, they tore my place apart. Chief Randall told me that the narcotics detectives read the address wrong and hit my apartment by mistake."

"What?"

"It's true. They tore my place apart. I know that they were looking for that shirt and that DNA report. Richard and Claudia are working together."

"Claudia is…was your boss at the paper wasn't she?"

"Yes. She's my friend too. We better hurry."

"Why would she be helping Richard?"

"Financial reasons. I'll explain it later."

"What are we doing?"

"I left the DNA report and the shirt in my rental car. Yesterday, someone vandalized my car while I was in Denten. It was towed to Pete's Garage. The insurance company was supposed to send someone out to look at it, and the rental company wanted it towed back to them. I phoned them after calling you, and they haven't sent anyone out there yet. I just hope that Claudia and Richard wait until tomorrow."

"While we get there tonight?"

"Right."

"This is overtime."

"What?"

"I'm going to have to charge you overtime."

"Jack, don't make my day any worse all right?"

"Nancy, you let me sue the city for the vandalism of your apartment, and I'll cut your bill right in half. It will be an easy win. I can get you anywhere from…"

"Jack, please. Just get me to Denten."

It was pitch dark when they reached Denten. "Watch out for deer," Nancy warned.

"I'm trying. Where's this place at?"

"We're almost there."

"So, you think the ex-mayor had something to do with his wife's murder?"

"Jack, it sounds that way. He wants that shirt and that DNA report, and he definitely doesn't want to have the case reopened. He said some really strange things. He kept saying, 'we did the right thing,' but he never said what they did or who they were."

"He told you to give him the shirt and the report?"

"No. He wanted to know where they were. He told me that when I found them, to give them to the Chief of Police."

"Ted Randall?"

"Right, that's the big buffoon that came to visit me today. He apologized for his men ripping my apartment apart."

"He'll be sorry all right when I take him to court."

"I think he's in on this too. What do you think?"

"He must be or why would Richard want you to give him the evidence? You said that you heard Richard talking on the phone to someone?"

"Right. He was telling someone not to hurt me. He told whomever it was that he was my friend and that he could talk to me and make me quit. He was waiting for me to come home so that he could tell me to quit writing the book."

"Nancy, aren't you afraid?"

"Yes, of course, I am, but I have to help Philip."

"Even if you might get killed doing it?"

"I'll share something with you, Jack. A long time ago, when I was a teenager, I did something that I regret, and I did this thing because my friends told me to. Well, when it was over, I realized that it was the wrong thing for me to do."

"What was the thing that you did?"

"It's not important. The point is, that there was this woman who talked to me about it, and she asked me, 'When you look in the mirror, who do you see?' And, I said, myself. She said, 'That's the person that you have to live with.' She was right Jack. I don't have to live with my friends or anyone else, but I always have to live with me."

"And so you have to help Philip because?"

"Because I have to. If I didn't, I would always know that I did the wrong thing. It's like I said Jack; I have to live with me. I would be a disappointment to myself, and then, well, how could I ever be happy?"

"Okay, my turn to give you advice. When you get killed and you look in the mirror, who do you see? Nobody, because you're dead. Now, how can you ever be happy? You can't."

"I believe in life after death, and so I would still be happy."

"I'd love to argue this further with you, but without a judge present, it just isn't worth it."

When they arrived at Pete's Garage, Nancy went up to the house and knocked on the door and then pounded. Minutes later, she watched Pete's large, tall frame stumble to the door. He opened it and focused his eyes on her. She was shocked by his appearance. Quickly, Nancy averted her eyes from his green striped boxer shorts and likewise from his naked chest. "I know it's late, but I left something in the trunk of my car."

"Come back tomorrow."

"I can't. It's very important."

"Give me a moment."

Nancy paced back and forth in the driveway until Pete returned to the door. Dressed in a pair of overalls and holding a set of keys and a flashlight, he made a beeline for the garage gate. After feeling for the padlock twice, he mumbled something and shined the flashlight in the direction where it should have been. It was missing. The gate was already open. He shoved it and opened it wider, and then he shined his flashlight on the ground and found the broken padlock.

Nancy waited next to Jack while Pete went back into the house. When Pete was once again standing at the open gate, Nancy asked him if he had gone into the house to phone the sheriff.

"No, I went to get my rifle."

She hadn't seen it when he came out of the house, but now, she couldn't stop seeing it. Its dark silhouette was leading the way for them.

Jack cleared his voice. "You know it's illegal to kill someone for trespassing. They have to actually be inside your house. It has to be self defense," Jack explained.

"I'm not going kill anyone," Pete said.

"Good," Jack sighed.

"I'm just gonna hurt them a little."

"Nancy, I think we better wait in my car."

"No, I want to see if they took the shirt and the DNA report."

She strode off catching up to Pete. Jack followed slowly behind them at a distance.

Pete noted that the lock on his garage door was broken too. He opened it and turned on the lights. Nancy started over towards the cars, but Pete reached out his big hand and grabbed onto her shoulder. "No, stay here. I have a guard dog that'll take off your face if you go near the vehicles."

He went farther into the garage. "Danger, Danger, where are you? Come on boy, come on out." He ran towards the back of the garage where he heard whimpering sounds.

The big, black Rottweiler lie panting and whimpering in a puddle of its own blood. "Someone stabbed him," Pete exclaimed, shocked that anyone could get near enough to the vicious dog to do it any harm.

Nancy ran towards Pete's voice but stopped short when she saw her white rental car. The trunk had been pried open and the edges of it were banged up. Jack was now standing beside Nancy. "Looks like they used a crowbar." He opened it, and they both looked inside at the empty trunk.

On the trip home, Nancy tried to understand how Claudia and Richard could do what they did. Jack broke through her thoughts. "Nancy. Earth calling Nancy."

"What?"

"Next time I tell you to keep quiet, do it. I told you that the sheriff didn't need to know anything, but you talked your head off. How do you know that Sheriff Cliff isn't in on it too?"

"It's Sheriff Clifford, and I didn't tell him that much."

"You told him that you suspected Richard Fellow."

"Jack, how am I going to help Philip now? That evidence was everything."

"No, not exactly. We could reopen the trial with Philip's medical records, a statement from the doctor, one from Mr. Nec, and even that witness you told me about, the one that only saw the back of his head. It'll just take a little longer without the solid evidence that's all."

"That's all?"

"Sorry."

"Jack, something is going on. The doctor in this town hid Philip's medical reports. Philip's attorney didn't defend him. Richard doesn't want evidence to be found that would clear Philip. There's a link somewhere. I just don't know where it is."

"It sounds like a conspiracy. For some reason they worked together to put Philip in prison."

"Exactly, but why? Why frame him? Why not try and catch the real murderer?"

"Maybe, you should ask Claudia some questions."

"I'm never talking to her again. She's no longer my friend. I know she wants to have her own newspaper and everything, but to sell me out like that. I just can't believe that she did that to me. How could she?"

Jack could hear Nancy's shaky voice, and he knew that she was upset. "Things will be all right." He patted her shoulder with a comforting hand.

CHAPTER 12

▼

CHASE

Nancy awoke to the sound of her phone ringing. She looked at her clock over by the window. It was 10:00 a.m. and raining outside. Pulling the receiver to her ear, she forced out a hello.

"Nancy?"

"Yes."

"This is Ellen Portson. How are you, dear?"

"Good, and how are you and Ed?"

"We're fine. I called because you left some things here."

"Things?" Nancy shot up into a sitting position on her bed. "What things?"

"An umbrella, a gym bag, an operator's manual for that rental car and two envelopes. One is large and one is small."

Now, Nancy recalled what she had done with the shirt and the DNA report. When her rental car had been vandalized, she had removed everything from the car and placed her things in the Portson's front room. She thanked God for her bouts of forgetfulness. It had saved her from telling Richard or Claudia where the envelopes were.

Nancy promised to visit Mrs. Portson by the afternoon. She just had no idea how she would do it without a car.

While she was sipping her hot tea and nibbling on pretzels, there was a quick steady knock at her door. She climbed up on her couch and looked through the peephole and saw a distorted image of Claudia. Quietly, she crept back over to her dining room table and sat back down. It was not until the knocking ceased that her nerves began to calm down. Moments later, she heard a loud thunk. It came from somewhere over by her balcony. She pulled back her curtains and looked at Claudia whose face was smashed up against the window. "Let me in! I've got something important to tell you."

Nancy immediately opened the door. "What are you doing out there? You're all wet. You could have slipped and fell. Are you nuts?"

"Why the hell didn't you answer the damn door?"

"Because you lied to me, Claudia."

"I know that. I've come over to tell you what happened. I didn't know that Richard was up to no good."

Nancy gave Claudia a towel to dry herself off. "I don't believe you."

"Listen. Richard phoned me yesterday and told me that if I wanted to keep you from getting yourself killed, then I needed to help him get that DNA report and that shirt from you. That's what he said, honest to God. Nancy, I didn't have a choice."

"I don't believe you, Claudia. I'll bet it was about money. He probably threatened to pull his money from your newspaper if you didn't get him that evidence."

"No. That's not true. I didn't get him the evidence. It wasn't in that trunk. I didn't know that he was going to break into that garage or hurt that dog."

"You helped him."

"Yes, I did. I did it for you though, and now I know it was wrong. Richard said that he'd do everything in his power to prevent Philip Secured from getting out of prison. When I told him about some of the stuff that you told me, he said that no matter what evidence you found, the truth would never change. He said, he knows that they did the right thing."

"They, who?"

"He wouldn't say."

"What did they do, setup Philip?"

"He didn't say, but it looks that way."

Nancy looked at Claudia's eyes. They looked sincere. She really didn't have much choice but to trust her. "I know where the DNA report and the shirt are. Will you drive me out to the Portsons?"

Claudia smiled, grateful to be back in Nancy's trust again. "Yes."

Nancy moved her couch and let Claudia exit through the doorway. She then pushed the couch back up against the door. After putting more water into Clansy's bowl, Nancy walked out onto her balcony, locked the balcony door, and climbed down the fire escape.

It did not take them long to reach Denten, not with Claudia driving. Claudia waited in her car while Nancy went inside of Ken Barton's store. Nancy waited in line behind a young boy and his parents. The parents paid for their items and carried their bags out to their truck. The boy lingered behind. He was holding his dollar and looking at all the different kinds of candy on the shelves up by the counter. "Come on, Brian," his father called to him.

Ken smiled. "He'll be fine, Mr. Robbin. I'll send him out as soon as he picks out his candy."

Nancy thought for a few seconds about the young boy's name, Brian Robbin. He's the boy who Dr. Kebler had to stitch up his toe. "How's your toe?"

"My toe?" The seven-year-old eyed her suspiciously.

"The one that you dropped the pickle jar on."

He looked at her as though she were strange. "I never dropped a pickle jar on my toe," he said and turned his attention back to the candy. "I want that candy bar in the corner." He paid Mr. Barton and ran out the door.

"Isn't that the boy who lives next door to the Portsons?"

"Yes." Ken answered giving her a puzzled look. "What's this about a pickle jar?"

"Oh, Dr. Kebler told me that he had to put some stitches in Brian Robbin's toe because he dropped a pickle jar on his foot."

"The doc's a liar. He's known for it."

"Why do you say that?"

"Take his wife for instance, nice, sweet person and very involved with the church. She was always helping people out, but him, he never helped anybody. He did just as much as a doctor had to do and no more. She convinced him to take patients who were poor, like Philip for instance. But, as soon as she left, he went back on his word. Any poor patients that he had accepted, he told them that he wouldn't see them anymore. He promised Mrs. Benton that he would vaccinate her child and that he'd accept a pig in return, but like I said, as soon as the doc's wife left, he went back on his word. The new born got sick and nearly died."

"That's awful."

"He's awful."

"Did he have some reason for not liking Philip?"

"No, but I heard that he didn't. Someone from the church told me that Helen…"

"Helen?"

"The doc's wife. They said that Helen was being painted by Philip, and her husband tried to make him stop. They snuck off somewhere, and Philip finished it. Right after that, Philip was arrested for killing that woman in the city, and Helen left to her mothers."

"Where does her mother live?"

"Minnesota. Helen still writes to my wife."

"I'd like to talk to Helen."

"I'll get you her phone number and her address. Hold on. Let me call my wife."

Within minutes, he handed Nancy a slip of paper with Helen's mother's information. It was one more piece to the puzzle that she was trying to solve. She returned to Claudia's car excited by the good luck that she had encountered.

"What took you so long?" Claudia snapped. "Were you in there making the root-beer and chips?"

"Very funny." Nancy handed Claudia a bottle of root-beer and a bag of chips. "Ken Barton, the store owner, was getting me Helen's mother's phone number and address. Helen is the doctor's wife."

"Yeah, so?"

"Drive and I'll tell you what happened." Nancy told her everything that Ken Barton had told her.

"Do you think that Philip and Helen were having an affair or something? Do you think that the doctor was jealous of Philip?"

"I don't know. I want to go and see Helen. Will you drop me off at the airport later?"

"Are you crazy? Just like that? You are going to go and see her?"

"I have to. I have to find out what happened. I have to prove that the doctor had a motive for framing Philip."

"I'll take you, but I hope you know what you're doing."

When Claudia drove up to the Portsons' house, she and Nancy saw Dr. Kebler's Mercedes parked in the driveway. Claudia parked directly behind it. "Now, what?"

"Stay here, Claudia, and keep the engine running."

"Hurry up."

Mr. Portson invited Nancy in. She went into the front room and straight up to Dr. Kebler, and as she had suspected, the envelopes were in his hands. Mrs. Portson smiled at Nancy. "There you are, dear. Doctor, I guess you won't need to give these to her later. Here she is."

"Yes, here I am."

Mrs. Portson tried to pull the two envelopes out of Dr. Kebler's hands. "Let me have them please."

"No."

Mrs. Portson was shocked.

"Dr. Kebler, those belong to me." Nancy no sooner said the words, and then she yanked the two envelopes from him. She turned and ran out of the room with them.

He ran after her up the stairs. "Nancy! You're not getting out of this house."

"What's going on Dr. Kebler?" sounded Mrs. Portson's voice following behind them.

Nancy looked out the window of the bathroom. She could see Claudia sitting out in her car staring up at the house. She opened the window. "Claudia! Claudia!"

Claudia put her window down more and stared harder at the house. She could hear her name. She exited her car and took a few steps near the house.

"Claudia, up here!"

She saw her just as Nancy threw the envelopes out of the window. "Get them, Claudia. Take them to Jack Stenson."

"What about you?"

Nancy heard the doorknob jiggling and then the loud kick against it. "Don't worry about me. Hurry up!" The door slammed open.

Claudia grabbed up the envelopes and ran to her car. She spun out of the driveway and raced down the road. Periodically, she checked her rearview mirror for the Mercedes. For nearly ten minutes, she saw nothing and assumed that she may make it out of

Denten, but then she heard the siren and saw the police car. She recognized the city sticker on the side of the vehicle, and she drove faster. Claudia cut down a winding road to the left and then a straight one to the right, but he was right behind her, so close that she was able to make out the Chief of Police, Ted Randall's face. She heard another siren on her right side and saw the sheriff's police car. She slammed on her brakes. The sheriff quickly made it over to her driver's side door. "Get out of the car!"

"I'm being chased."

"I said get out of the car!"

She got out and put her hands up above her head.

"Lower your arms. I want to see your driver's license and registration. Do you know how fast you were going?"

"What? Sheriff, I was being chased by him," she said pointing to Chief Randall as he approached the vehicle.

"I'm glad you finally stopped my criminal."

"Your what?"

"My criminal. I have to take her in for questioning. She stole something. These envelopes," he said reaching his hand into her car.

Sheriff Clifford took a step towards him and blocked his way. "You're not taking anything or anyone."

"I'm the Chief of Police," he said with authority in his voice.

"Not around here you're not. Around here, you're a driver who was speeding, and I'm giving you a ticket next so don't you go anywhere."

"The hell you are."

"Now, you're getting another one for disrespecting an officer of the law."

"I have a right to chase my criminal."

"And just where did she steal these envelopes from?"

"That's none of your business."

"If she stole them from some place here in Denten, then it is my business and not yours. Do you want to press charges? I'll do an investigation. I'll take you both down to the station. If not, then you get back over by your car and wait for your tickets."

Chief Randall marched back over to his car and made a phone call. The sheriff watched him and as soon as he was out of earshot, he directed his attention to Claudia. "Nancy called me and told me that you were being chased by Dr. Kebler. I didn't expect Chief Randall to be after you. Why does he want the envelopes?"

"They have evidence in them that will prove Philip Secured is innocent."

"I'll hold him up as long as I can. That should get you out of Denten. You're on Rock Road. Take a left up at the corner and just keep going straight. That will take you to the highway. The doctor's still out there somewhere so be careful."

Claudia sped off, but as she drove out of the sheriff's sight, she was once again being followed. This time it was by Richard Fellow in his Mark VIII. She went as fast as she could, and as she turned near a field, she flung the envelopes out into a ditch. All she could see was a big sign that read, NO HUNTING. That would be the only landmark that she could give to Jack Stenson.

She outraced Richard but stayed in Denten. She knew that the chief's phone call was to other squad cars, and if she left Denten, she would be picked up. Miraculously, she found her way to Ken Barton's store. She ran in and used his phone. Jack Stenson promised her that he would come out to Denten right away. She hoped that he'd be able to find Rock Road and the no hunting sign and the two envelopes. Claudia phoned Nancy at the Portsons' with the help of Ken Barton who knew everybody's phone number in town.

"Nancy, calm down. I'm fine. I put the envelopes somewhere safe. Stenson's going to pick them up. Do you want me to come and get you?"

Nancy paced back and forth in the kitchen. "No. I'm going to the airport."

"You better be careful. Ted Randall's out there and so is Richard. They were both chasing me."

After saying good-bye to Claudia, Nancy put on the farmer hat and tightened the big blue overalls. She climbed up on the tractor, and Mrs. Portson handed her the brown paper bag to hide her purse in. Nancy turned the key and thrust the lever to drive.

Nearing the little church in town, she spotted Richard standing out by his car. He was conversing with Chief Randall and Dr. Kebler who were both standing by their cars. Her head lowered to hide her face beneath the hat as she bounced past them on the bumpy dirt road.

Pete saw the tractor and phoned Mrs. Portson. "She's here." He hung up the receiver quickly and climbed into his truck.

As soon as she reached Pete's driveway, she turned off the engine, jumped off the tractor, and ran to Pete's truck. "Thanks for helping me." Pete merely nodded as she climbed into the passenger side. "How's your dog?"

"The vet said that Danger needs to rest until his stitches are out. Whoever did that to him is going to be sorry," he assured her in an angry voice.

She nodded her understanding, but did not divulge any information. They were silent the rest of the way to the airport.

CHAPTER 13

▼

HELEN KEBLER

As the airplane flew out from under the clouds, Nancy was able to see the little houses and trees, the tiny swimming pools and business buildings, and the miniature cars and trucks. She thought of how manageable things looked from a distance. From here, the world looked so fictional. You could pretend that everyone was living happily.

After a short taxi ride, she was ringing the doorbell of Helen Kebler's mother's house. A young pretty woman answered, and Nancy recognized her from the portrait in Dr. Kebler's home. Nancy had already thought the introduction through while she was on the plane. A quick, honest explanation for her visit was what she thought would work best.

"Helen, hello. My name is Nancy Mead. I'm a friend of Philip Securd. Ken Barton who runs the store in Denten said that you and Philip were friends and that you probably wouldn't mind answering a few questions for me."

Helen was smiling, but her eyes were large and giving off a look of surprise. She backed away from the door and at the same time, she invited Nancy into the house. "What kind of questions?" she asked in a thin, soft voice.

"Oh, just a few simple ones. I'm trying to help Philip get a new trial."

"A new trial?"

Nancy saw Helen's hand tremble and her peachy color drain from her face. She was now pasty white and shaky. "P P Please, have a seat. I was just on my way to the church picnic."

Nancy thought she had a pretty smile, just like the one that Philip had captured in his portrait of her. "Ken Barton told me that you used to be a nun."

"Yes, that's true. Would you like something to drink? We have tea, coffee, and milk. I think we have some soda."

"Tea will be fine, thank you. Do you know Richard Fellow?"

"He's my husband's cousin. They're very close, almost like brothers."

Nancy saw puzzle pieces fitting together. One big clear piece of the picture revealed itself. "What about Chief Ted Randall?"

"His name sounds familiar, but I don't know him."

"How well did you know Philip Secured?"

Helen's hand that held the sugar bowl began to tremble uncontrollably. "Well," she uttered nervously.

"Are you all right?"

"Yes, I'm fine. Thank you."

"I'm sorry for upsetting you, but I must know if you believe that Philip killed Jane Fellow."

Nancy watched her take a deep breath as she lowered herself into a chair opposite hers. "I...I don't. He couldn't have. Not Philip, he was just too sweet."

"Your husband had some medical records on Philip: records that I think he deliberately hid during the trial. No one knew that Philip was suffering with a brain tumor."

Nancy watched Helen's face change from tight tense muscles to that of drowned sorrow. Her eyes seemed to swell instantly with tears, and all at once, she was crying. "I told him not to lie. God save his soul."

"Your husband's?"

Helen tried to choke out a word but failed. Nodding her head was all that she could manage.

"Tell me about it."

Her eyes grew huge. Nancy could read the fear in them. "Helen, I know this is difficult for you, but Philip needs your help. Today, his lawyer has some new evidence that will get him a new trial. It's strong evidence, but it's not enough to free him from prison."

Helen cried harder and nodded her head in agreement. "I know. I know. Oh, the guilt I've lived with. Oh, God forgive me. God forgive my husband."

Nancy knew now that she was about to hear the true story of what happened to Jane Fellow. "It's going to be all right. Just tell me what happened."

"Where do I begin? How do I begin? It's all so dreadful."

Nancy took her hand. It was small and very light. Her eyes held more innocence in them than that of a child's. If she was guilty of anything, no one would ever know by looking into her eyes. Nancy looked at Helen's angelic face with the soft skin and the big doe eyes and felt overwhelmed by her appearance of purity. The reflection from the kitchen lights shone upon Helen's brown hair and created a halo shaped glow around the crown of her head. Nancy felt her hand grow warm from the heat of Helen's. Nancy thought she was experiencing the flow of goodness in the spiritual sense. She had heard plenty of stories about all the good deeds that Helen had done for others, and it made her miserable to upset her. How can I hurt such a wonderful person, she thought. "I'm awfully sorry to upset you like this. Please, try to relax. Take your time."

"He never liked Philip. He said that there was something odd about him. Oh, God save his soul. God forgive him."

"Forgive him for what, Helen? What did he do?"

"I told Keith that there was nothing wrong with Philip. He's a good boy I told him. I really liked Philip."

"He's very likable."

"His mother died when he was just an infant."

"Yes, I know."

"He had special needs that weren't met when he was young, and I tried to help him. I used to hold Philip on my lap and let him pretend that he was an infant and that I was his mother."

Nancy winced at the image that she was conjuring up. Philip was only a few years younger than Helen was. What in the world is she saying? Philip at his age and sitting on her lap! She shifted in her seat and at the same time managed to pull her hand away from Helen's. Nancy didn't like to think of herself as a judgmental type of person. Quickly, she thought of a way out for Helen. Perhaps, Helen was into psychiatry and this was therapeutic for Philip.

"One day when Philip was visiting me, Keith caught him sitting on my lap, and he thought the worst. He was a bit perverse."

Nancy nodded her head in agreement, but was not sure if she was agreeing with what Keith had been thinking or with what Helen was saying. She continued to lean forward in her seat and listen intently.

"We weren't doing anything wrong. He was just sitting on my lap, and I was rocking him. Philip's bigger than me, so he had to straddle me. He had to sit with his butt between my legs on the chair and hang his legs over the sides. I guess it looked strange. We couldn't see ourselves, so I don't really know how it looked. Keith yelled at us and pounded on Philip with his fists. I managed to stop him. Philip wasn't allowed over to visit me anymore."

"When did this happen?"

"About a month before Jane was murdered."

"How long had you and Philip been…um….been…rocking…in the chair?"

"Years."

"Years?" Nancy was shocked by the information, and she realized that it must have registered on her face because Helen followed it up with an explanation.

"I don't really remember how that began. It was just a thing we did. It made us feel good. It was completely innocent."

Then why is your face turning so red? Nancy tried to imagine rocking with a grown man in a chair in the position that Helen had described. A good healthy bit of physical activity; a comforting, relaxing therapeutic exercise; or just a unique enjoyable way for two people to move together: plenty of innocent explanations. Nancy decided that it mostly depended on what thoughts that the participants were having at the time.

"What did you two think about when you were rocking?"

Helen's lips pursed together tightly, and her eyes narrowed. "That's none of your business."

Nancy backed off. "Sorry." She waited a few minutes and then asked, "Did Philip know Jane Fellow?"

"I don't know. She saw a painting of me and wanted a portrait of herself for her husband. I gave her Philip's address. I don't know if she ever contacted him or not."

"I saw that portrait at your house."

"No, you couldn't have."

"It was hanging on the wall in the living room."

She looked appalled by the thought. "That! No. That thing was painted years ago by someone far less talented. The one Philip painted is here with me."

"May I see it?"

After an awkward moment of silence, she said, "It's in my bedroom. Follow me."

Nancy stood in awe at the picture. It was huge, practically covering half of one wall. It was of Helen from head to toe and completely nude. Her long flowing hair covered parts of her shoulders and her breasts.

"Oh, that's...that's not at all what I expected. I haven't seen any of Philip's paintings look like this. I mean it's beautiful, but I can hardly believe that Philip painted this."

"It was his first painting like this. I was his very first nude model."

"What did your husband think?"

"Hated it. He tried to stop us."

"Why?"

"I don't know. It's innocent. It's art."

"Was he jealous of Philip?"

"Very much."

They returned to the kitchen. Helen took a long drink of water. She eyed Nancy suspiciously. "Why are you here?"

"I told you, I'm trying to help Philip."

"Why?"

"I think he's innocent."

"Why do you care about him?"

"He asked for my help."

"So, you just helped him?"

Nancy wondered if Helen was jealous of her. "Yes, I did. Ken Barton, at the store, said that you used to help people in town all the time. Why did you do that?"

"I care about people."

"So do I."

"Did Philip ask about me?"

Nancy wanted Helen's help so desperately that one white lie seemed in order. "Yes, he did."

Helen smiled. After a long moment of silence, she began to give up more puzzle pieces. Her voice took on a depressing tone. "The night that Jane was murdered, they came to our door."

"Who?"

"Richard and a man that I'd never seen before. They were very serious about something. I heard them mention Philip's name. I was told to go back to bed, but I slipped into the kitchen instead, and I listened. I heard Keith say that he would help Richard. Then, they went out to Keith's office."

"You mean his doctor's office?"

"Yes, I didn't know what they were doing at the time. Not until later."

"What were they doing?"

"Keith was giving Richard and that other man Philip's blood. He had drawn some of his blood earlier that week for tests."

"When did you find out that Keith gave it to them?"

"The next morning. That's when I was packaging up the test tubes of blood to be sent to the lab, and I noticed that Philip's was missing. Hours later, I heard that Philip was arrested and that his blood had been found at the crime scene."

"Did you question your husband about it?"

"Yes, but he said that I wouldn't understand. I couldn't stay with him knowing that he did that."

"So you moved here. Why didn't you tell someone?"

"Who was I going to tell?"

"Philip's lawyer."

"Philip's lawyer, Gary Saster? He used to come over on the weekends and watch football games with Keith and Richard. They are as close as brothers."

"What?"

"I'm afraid that it's true."

"How did Philip's fingerprints wind up at the crime scene?"

"Someone transferred them."

"Who?"

"I don't know. I think that guy that Richard was with. I heard him say that he'd take care of the transfer of prints. I thought that they were talking about pictures. I heard him say something about tape, and I just thought that the pictures were torn or something. I had no idea what they were about to do to Philip until they had done it."

"What about that witness, Josephine Wilderk?"

"She was a crack addict. I know. I used to do an awful lot of charity work in the big city before I moved to Denten, and she was always in trouble with the law. She lost all five of her children. State took them."

"She said that they were living with their fathers."

"She didn't even know their fathers. She did things for money to buy her drugs. Children for her were a side effect."

"You knew her personally?"

"Yes, I did."

"Then, you knew she was a bought witness?"

"No, I thought she was lying, but I had no way of knowing if someone paid her to lie, and I still have no way of knowing that."

"I have a way to prove that she was lying. This witness, Mr. Nec, he met Jane Fellow at a store on the night that she was murdered. It was at nine o'clock. Joephine said that she saw Jane being murdered at eight o'clock. Jane's blood was on Mr. Nec's shirt. That'll prove that she was still alive an hour after Josephine said that she saw her being murdered."

Nancy took a sip of her tea. She could tell by Helen's continual glances at the clock on the kitchen wall that she wished that she would leave, but the picture to the puzzle was only a flat one. It lacked the depth it needed in order to be understood.

"Why did they frame Philip?"

"I don't know. After I had figured it out, I went to Keith, and I told him what I knew. He denied it, and then when I started crying, he told me that he wished that he could tell me the reason why, but that I would never understand. He said that he did not want me to have to share in his guilt."

"But you did."

"Yes, I did."

"And you still are. As long as you know about what they did, you are as guilty as they are unless you come forward. Will you testify at Philip's new trial?"

"No, not against my husband."

"You're separated."

"We'll always be married. I don't believe in divorce."

"There's an innocent man sitting in prison."

"He's in the hospital isn't he?"

"For now, yes. How did you know?"

"Mrs. Barton and I keep in touch. She knows how fond I am of Philip."

"Do you miss him?"

"Oh, yes. I cry often when I think of Philip suffering."

"Do you know who might have killed Jane Fellow?"

"No, I don't."

"Did she have any enemies?"

"No."

"Are you sure that Philip couldn't have done it?"

"I'm absolutely sure. Philip could never hurt anyone."

"You've got to testify if you want to help Philip."

"I can't."

"I'll subpoena you."

"My husband said that he was doing what was right. I trust him."

"That's why you're living here with your mother? That's why you've asked God to forgive him, to bless his soul and so on. If that's true, why are you feeling so guilty?"

"It's because…"

"It's because you are."

Helen's face was completely red and her eyes were the size of tiny slits. "I would like you to leave now."

Nancy headed for the door. "Oh, I will, but we'll see each other again, because I will subpoena you, and you will be in court."

"I won't show up."

"You'll go to jail if you don't. They may even send you to prison."

"Then, I'll go to prison."

Nancy stood at the door. "Helen, your husband framed Philip, and you are just as guilty because you let him get away with putting an innocent man in prison."

"He said I wouldn't understand about what he had to do, and I don't. No, I don't think that it was right, but he's my husband. God's word is that a wife shall obey her…"

"What about though shall not lie?"

"I want you to leave."

"I want you to testify."

"No."

"If you care about Philip, you have to."

Nancy saw Helen's face contort, full of frustration. Her loyalties were divided, and she seemed void of an inner voice.

"Helen, how can you sleep at night?"

Helen pulled the door open. "Good bye."

Nancy left reluctantly. Even though she had heard the door slam shut behind her, she hoped that perhaps something that she had said today would work its way into Helen's conscience.

C H A P T E R   14

▼

FRAMED

Days later, after Nancy's visit with Helen Kebler, Jack Stenson filed a court appeal in Philip Securd's behalf. Nancy sighed relief when Jack told her that Philip's appeal was being pushed up, in front of a long line of other criminal appeal cases because of his illness. In a couple of months, Philip would have his chance to be found not guilty, and those who had framed him would be discovered. The conspiracy would be revealed, and the reason behind it would be known. Nancy would soon have the 3-D puzzle solved, and her mind could rest. Philip would be back home with the Portsons if everything worked out as Nancy expected it to.

Nancy's couch was back in place against the wall in her living room. The door was now fixed and everything appeared to be the way it was before the narcotics raid on her apartment. She walked out of her bedroom wearing a blue nightgown. In one hand she had her pillow, and in the other, a thin small blanket. Nancy lay on the couch and closed her eyes. The ticking of her watch nagged at her until she sat up and removed it from her wrist. Once again, she tried to close her eyes and rest, but this time it was the buzzing sound of her refrigerator that bothered her. "It's no good," she said sitting up.

Her cat uncurled himself from the end of the couch where he had been asleep.

"I can't sleep, Clansy." Seeing the time appear in bright glowing numbers on her watch that was on the coffee table, aggravated her even more. "One o'clock in the morning. When am I ever going to get some sleep?" She knew the answer to that before she even asked the question. She would not sleep peacefully until that trial was over, and it had not begun yet. Turning the lights back on in the living room, Nancy whined, "I can't sleep in my bedroom. I can't sleep out here. I can't sleep anywhere. Oh, Clansy, what am I going to do?"

"Hot chocolate sounds good. Why not caffeine? I can't sleep anyway. Good idea, Clansy." She looked at the phone and thought about calling and talking to someone. No one would be up, and who ever did answer the phone, she knew would yell at her for calling so late. "Come on, Clansy, let's go into the kitchen. I'll make you some warm milk."

On her way into the kitchen, there was a knock at her apartment door. She crept over to her door and looked through the peephole. It was Richard.

"Nancy?" He knocked a few more times. He looked through the peephole at her.

She backed up so fast that she almost stepped on her cat. She quickly stopped her foot from landing on Clansy and immediately shifted her weight to step over him, but he moved to her next step, and she fell right next to the door.

Richard's voice held assurance in it. "Nancy, please. I need to talk to you. It's important."

Nancy pulled herself up. "Go away, Richard. I don't trust you."

"I know that you don't, but, Nancy, please, let me talk to you. I'm trying to save your life."

"Richard, go away."

"Not until I've told you what I've come to say."

"No. I'm not letting you in. I'm going to my bedroom, Richard, and you had better leave, or I'll call the police." Nancy strode off to her bedroom realizing that the threat to call the police was hollow since the chief of the department was apparently his best friend and a major part of the conspiracy to frame Philip. She sat on her bed and thought about what it was Richard had come to say to her. He wants to save my life. What does he mean? Is someone trying to kill me? Doesn't he realize that if someone were trying to kill me, I would suspect it to be him?

Nancy approached her apartment door again. "Richard?"

"Yes."

"I'm going to call Claudia. If she comes over, I'll let you in to talk to me."

"That's really unnecessary, Nancy. I'm not going to hurt you, but if that's what you think, then go ahead and have her come over."

Nancy phoned Claudia and reached her answering machine. "Claudia, pick up. This is Nancy. Pick up. Claudia, wake up and answer your phone." She hung up and called again. The answering machine clicked on once more. Nancy left the same message.

She phoned for the third time, and Claudia answered. "Nancy, what the hell do you want? This better be important."

"I'm sorry to wake you up so late, but Richard is outside my door, and he wants to come in and talk to me. I told him that I would let him in if you came over."

"When?"

"Now."

"What?"

"Claudia!"

"Tell him to come back later when I'm awake."

"He said that he's not leaving from my door."

"What?"

"That's what he said."

"So, let him rot out there."

"Claudia, he said that he wanted to tell me something that would save my life."

"I'll stay on the phone with you, and you let him in."

"No, what if he tries to kill me or something?"

"Richard's a liar, not a murderer."

"How do you know?"

"Nancy, just let him in. If he tries anything, I'll call the police for you."

"How are you going to do that if we're on the line together?"

"Hold on."

Claudia returned to the phone. "Now, I've got my cell phone next to me. Go ahead and let him in."

"Great, now you can listen to me die on one phone while you call for help on the other. I'll be dead by the time the police arrive because you were too lazy to come over."

"Oh, don't be silly. If Richard wanted to kill you, he wouldn't wait outside your apartment door until you let him in. If he wanted to kill you, he would have broken down your door by now and done it. He certainly wouldn't have knocked and alerted you like he did. Now, go let him in. I'll stay on the phone."

Nancy put on a silky pink robe and carried her phone over to the apartment door. "Richard, I'm going to let you in, but if you try something, Claudia is going to phone the police." So, don't kill me, she thought.

Richard rushed in and briskly headed for her bathroom. "I'll be right back," he said.

Nancy lifted the phone to her mouth. "He went to the bathroom. I'm in the kitchen. Stay on the line with me." Nancy poured the container of milk, filling up Clansy's saucer. Then, she poured the last of the milk into her favorite Snoopy cup. She placed the cup into the microwave. When the timer went off, Nancy carefully removed her cup. Slowly, she stirred in the cocoa, letting the chocolate aroma rise up to sooth her. Her expectations of tasting the sweet drink heightened.

Richard was standing before her when she turned towards the recycling bin with the empty milk container. His unexpected presence frightened her, and she screamed.

"Sorry, I didn't mean to scare you." He picked up the Snoopy cup. "Thanks for the hot chocolate." He saw the bowl of warm milk on the counter and understood that she was in the middle of feeding her cat. "I'll wait for you over on the couch," he said on his way into the living room.

She remembered the clutched phone in her hand. "Claudia?"

"I called the police. Are you all right?"

"Yes, I'm fine. Cancel your call."

"But I heard you scream."

"It was an accident. I'm fine."

"What do you mean an accident?"

"Richard came around the corner, and I didn't know he was there."

"Hold on." Claudia returned to the phone. "Do you know how hard it is to explain why you dialed 911 by accident?"

"Sorry." Nancy bent down and gave Clansy his milk. "I won't let it happen again, Claudia."

Nancy went into the living room and sat at the farthest end of the couch away from Richard. He scooted near her. "You don't want any hot chocolate?"

"No," she lied, craving to sip the sweet drink slowly and savor the taste.

"Mmmm, it's delicious." He gulped the warm chocolate drink in seconds and set the empty mug on the coffee table. "Nancy, I won't keep you in suspense." Richard locked his eyes with hers. "Philip Secud is an extremely dangerous man, and if you help him get out of prison, you may be one of his victims. Nancy, do you know how hard it is for me to even mention his name? He killed my wife. What do you think it's like for me Nancy?"

"Richard, I don't think Philip did it, and when we go to trial, you'll find out why. Richard, you're going to feel bad about what you did. You set him up, and you were wrong."

"I'm not denying that. I know I set him up. We all did, but we did it for a reason, Nancy. He did murder Jane, but he was clever. He didn't leave one fingerprint, not even one piece of evidence. We had to do what we did to save other women's lives. Women like you Nancy: innocent women who like to think the best of everybody; women who believe that no nice boy like Philip Secud is a murderer."

"You admit that you framed him, you and your cousin, Dr. Kebler? You two and that defense lawyer, Gary Saster, and Chief Ted Randall? All of you were in on it. Right? That's everybody isn't it? Oh, no, I almost forgot Josephine Wilderk. Richard, how could you? How could they? Why? Why did you frame Philip?"

"I told you. You're not listening. He did it. He murdered her." He sighed and shook his head. "Listen to me, Nancy." He knelt down on his knees in front of her. "Do you honestly think that I would send an innocent man to prison?"

"How could he have murdered her? He couldn't even drive. How did he get into the city that night?"

"Nancy, he hitchhiked into the city, and who knows why he killed her. Maybe he didn't think that she paid him enough for the painting. I don't know the reason. I just know that he did it. Ask Keith. He knew what Philip was like."

"What painting?"

Nancy watched Richard wipe back tears. "He killed her, Nancy. She went there to see him because my cousin's wife told her that he would paint her portrait. It was going to be a present for me, a surprise gift to celebrate my running for governor. I loved her, Nancy, more than any woman in the world." Richard was now crying openly.

Nancy went to the bathroom and returned to the living room with a box of tissue. After a few moments had passed, she asked, "How did you know about the portrait if it was a secret?"

"My cousin told me about it."

"When?"

"The night that Jane was murdered. He also told me that Philip had tried to hurt his wife before, and he had to stop him. Keith said that Philip goes crazy sometimes. It's true, Nancy. He killed Jane."

"Prove it, Richard."

"I can't. He covered his tracks. The only way to punish him was to do what we did."

"Whose idea was it, Richard?"

"It was Keith's."

"Richard, the truth is going to come out in court. You're all going to pay for what you did."

"I know that, Nancy, but that's not why I'm here. I'm here to warn you. You don't know what you're doing."

"Please go, Richard."

"If you do this, you are going to put a lot of women in danger, including yourself."

"Richard, I heard what you had to say. Now, I'm asking you to leave."

He looked at the phone in her hand. "You're right, Nancy. You gave me your time. I'll go."

After he left, Nancy felt shaky. "Claudia, did you hear what he said?" Nancy yelled, "Claudia!"

"What? What?" she mumbled.

"Were you sleeping?"

"No. No. What?"

"You were sleeping. I could've been killed."

"You weren't. What did Richard say?"

"I'll tell you tomorrow. Go back to sleep."

"I'll be over around ten."

"Good night, Claudia."

Nancy hung up the phone. The one thing on her mind now was the portrait of Jane. Where was it, and how did Dr. Kebler know about it when not even his wife knew about it? Helen said that she didn't know if Jane had even contacted Philip. If Philip was painting Jane, why didn't he say something about it?

CHAPTER 15

▼

JUSTIFIED CONSPIRACY

Months later, during Philip Secured's trial, the words justified conspiracy became part of the public's everyday language. Justified conspiracy was now the only weapon the law had in dealing with the smart, calculating criminals like Philip Secured.

Nancy sat down on her couch feeling the weight of the trial. The misery that she felt was deepened by Claudia's abundance of energetic excitement. Claudia bounced onto the couch. With a big smile she announced, "Finally, my little newspaper is competition for *The Doverlaine Daily*. Give me an interview."

"No, Claudia. I can't."

"After all I've done for you, Nancy, this is the least that you could do for me."

"It doesn't feel right."

"My paper is selling like fire because of this trial."

"I can't believe that Richard hasn't pulled his money on you."

"Well, he hasn't, and he's been kind enough to give me an interview."

"He shouldn't have. None of them should have. They're all crooked, and they keep pointing their dirty rotten fingers at Philip trying to convince people that he is guilty. It's horrifying. What they did could happen to anybody. It could happen to you, Claudia: a doctor takes your blood to the crime scene, your lawyer doesn't defend you, a woman is paid to testify that she saw you commit the murder, and a policeman transfers your fingerprints to the crime scene after he arrests you. How would you like it, Claudia, if it happened to you?"

"Great stuff, Nancy. Let me quote you on that. Now, tell me why you wanted to help Philip Securd?"

"I'm not giving you an interview, Claudia."

"Look, Nancy, you just said that the conspirators are justifying their actions by accusing Philip of murdering Jane. It's true that they have no proof that he murdered her, and what evidence they do have, they created. So, let's hear your side of it. Tell the public why it's wrong. Use that guilt thing that you just did on me for an example. Get your point across, Nancy. Defend Philip in the public's eye."

"Fine, quote me."

"Great. I'll send you a free copy."

"Fine."

Claudia saw a copy of her newspaper on Nancy's coffee table. "Yesterday's paper was a sell out." She picked up the *News To Know* and looked at the front cover. "Richard's looking like a hero. That speech he gave in court about being tired of criminals getting away with murder was spectacular. It was like one of those famous speeches from our forefathers or something. He had enough of it, the criminals outsmarting the honest, innocent people, and he was willing to take a stand against it, even if it meant replanting the dirt and risking his own freedom as he had done. He said it was worth it as long as he saved honest, innocent lives. He said he would do it all over again in the name of his dead wife who was murdered by such garbage as Philip Secured."

"Claudia, stop it! It's wrong. He has no proof that Philip murdered his wife. I hope the jury is not as gullible as you and Richard's idiotic followers."

"Idiotic?"

"They're stupid, Claudia. If it can happen to Philip, and it did, it can happen to them. It can happen to you and me."

"Today, another doctor is going to testify."

"Claudia, I don't want to talk about this trial anymore. It's making me sick the way everyone is justifying a conspiracy against Philip."

Nancy held out her hand to Claudia, and Claudia gave her the newspaper that she was holding. Nancy walked into her kitchen and threw it into the garbage can. Claudia frowned. "I'm sorry, Nancy, I didn't mean to upset you."

Nancy nodded her head. "I know. Claudia, I haven't had a chance to thank you for hiring me on your newspaper staff. If you hadn't done that, the dealership wouldn't have sold me my new car."

"Don't even mention it, Nancy. Here's some good news. This should make you feel better. *The Doverlaine Daily* is ending its strike, and now they want to buy me out."

"Are you going to sell?"

"Not right now. I'm going to let them squirm for a while until my money runs out. I have a few of their clients buying ads from me, and that's what has them worried."

"I guess they'll be calling everyone back to work then."

"Yes, they will. Until then, you're still working for me, right?"

"Right."

"You'll continue to cover the trial for me?"

"Yes. I will."

After Claudia left, Nancy fed her cat and got ready to go. She packed up her laptop and headed to the courthouse.

Before court was in session, Nancy had a moment to speak to Philip's attorney just outside the doors to the courthouse. "Jack, what's going on here? They're proudly admitting that they framed Philip, and every one is cheering them on."

"I know. Calm down."

"Jack?"

"It's Richard running for governor; it's the Chief of Police. These are important people. I can't explain how they can make crime sound like a good thing, but they can, and they have. It'll change though. As soon as we prove that Philip couldn't have murdered Jane, everything will change."

"I hope so."

Nancy walked slowly into the courtroom and took her usual seat, the one that she had been sitting in from the start of the trial. Everyday she heard more testimonies and with each one, the puzzle of Philip's conviction became more complete.

Today, more experts were coming into court to explain their theories about what causes Philip to experience rages, forgetfulness, and blackouts. It was hard to follow anything that they were saying. The medical terminology was above her understanding, as it was everyone else's in the courtroom, including the judge's. The definitions provided were given by the doctors, who clearly made poor teachers, taking turns to drone over dry material that they read from a textbook. Nothing Nancy could remember had ever been this boring, not even the time that she had counted ceiling tiles for six hours inside of a stuck elevator.

The judge had allowed Dr. Kebler's testimony about Philip's rage and his blackouts to become the main focus of the trial when the knowledge was pointless because they were supposed to be proving that Philip received an unfair trial. Nancy thought about the judge and decided that idiots are sometimes voted into places where they don't belong, like behind a bench in a courtroom.

Nancy typed a few more words into her laptop about how none of this testimony mattered. Then, she exited the file and opened older files to read some of the testimonies that were heard at the start of the trial. She now let her mind concentrate on previous information about Philip's case.

When Richard had taken the witness stand, he told the jury that his cousin, Dr. Keith Kebler, had phoned him a little after 10:00 p.m. to say that he thought Jane's life was in danger. His cousin had also told him that Philip Secur'd was a dangerous man, and that he had tried to hurt Helen. Hours later, Chief Randall came to his house and broke the sad news to him that Jane's body had been found in an alley in the city. The quick investigation by the police at the scene uncovered no evidence. Richard and Chief Randall then went to Keith Kebler's house. They wanted to find out what he knew. Richard admitted to the jury that he was irrational and wanted revenge. He wanted to kill Philip.

When Dr. Kebler had his turn on the witness stand, he had told the jury that Philip suffered from black outs in which he experienced fits of rage, and because he had nearly killed Helen during one, he forbid Philip to see Helen. He testified that he had convinced Richard to work with him on punishing Philip by making certain that he was found guilty of murdering Jane. He admitted that he sprinkled Philip's blood from the test tube all over the alley where Jane's body had been found.

Chief of Police, Ted Randall, admitted to transferring Philip's fingerprints from the police station to the crime scene. A day later, after the body had been removed from the alley, the fingerprints had been planted.

Mr. and Mrs. Portson, Sheriff Clifford, and Ken Barton had all taken the stand as character witnesses for Philip. From their descriptions, it was clear that Philip was a nice boy who helped people out. He was a slow learner but a committed worker at the store; a young man suffering with a brain tumor and yet a gifted artist; one with an orphan upbringing who had no regrets or anger over his unfortunate childhood. He was the boy who beat the odds and developed into a nice young man.

Nancy looked up from her computer and took a second to focus on the present testimony. The author of one of the dry textbooks was now taking the stand. Just when she didn't think it could get more boring, the king of drone was taking his turn.

She returned her attention to the old files on her laptop. When Attorney Jack Stenson had subpoenaed Attorney Gary Saster, he was able to prove that Gary was one of Robert Fellow's and Keith Kebler's best friends. He too, admitted to his part in the conspiracy. Gary Saster simply did not do his job to defend Philip.

Josephine Wilderk was another witness that Jack had subpoenaed to court. He was able to get her to confess that she had been paid by Attorney Gary Saster to testify that she saw a murder in the alley that night. She said that she actually did see the murder and had only lied about the time that it took place and the description of the man. She stated that she did see shadows in the alley of a man stabbing a woman and that she did hear screams. Josephine described the screams as three low deep sounds. She saw the shadows and heard the screams that night close to 10:00 o'clock, not 8:00 o'clock.

Mr. Nec took the stand after Josephine Wilderk. The time of Jane's death was changed because her DNA was found on Mr. Nec's shirt. Jane was with Mr. Nec just before she was murdered. The man chasing her could have been Philip since the time frame of Jane's death was only two hours later than what Josephine had stated at the first trial. Unfortunately, Philip still had no alibi.

Helen Kebler's testimony came after Robert Fellow's and Chief Ted Randall's. Her testimony was serving to confirm theirs. The most important question she answered for the defense was about Philip being dangerous. Did she think that Philip was dangerous? She answered no. Did your husband think that Philip was dangerous? She answered that she didn't know, but yes it was true that she was forbidden to see Philip. Was your husband jealous of Philip? She said that he did not understand art. The portrait of her was brought in and marked as a piece of evidence. Observers and even the jury members murmured comments and sounds of praise. Pleased by the artwork, nearly everyone had smiled except for Dr. Kebler. His eyebrows were lowered, lips pursed, and his face red. Upon his face was a mixture of embarrassment and anger.

When Jack Stenson had asked Helen about an activity involving a rocking chair, she had gasped for air and had fallen forward in her seat. The court took a long recess after that.

Helen's husband's testimony that Philip Securd's illness caused him to commit uncontrollable acts of rage and not remember them caused the most commotion in the courtroom. What brought on this rage was now the question consuming the entire trial.

Nancy heard the judge say that the court was taking a break for lunch. She looked up from the screen of her laptop in time to see the judge yawn. Quickly, she closed the old files and shut down her computer. In seconds, she was at her car. Nancy jumped into the driver seat and phoned Claudia on her cell phone.

"I'm begging you, Claudia. This is boring. Give it to Jimmy or someone. Let me have a break from this. It's been three days now of listening to medical experts and psychologist, and now they're putting authors on the stand. This is ridiculous."

Disappointed with Claudia's decision, Nancy drove past the restaurant that she knew her friend, Jack Stenson, ate at regularly. She just couldn't stomach listening to anything more about the trial.

Sinking to depression, she drove to the nearest theater, went in, and watched a movie about war.

Nancy returned to the courtroom ten minutes late and braced herself for more tiresome testimony. The rest of the court day drug on until finally it was over. She left with no energy.

When she returned home, she flopped onto the couch, not even bothering to change her clothes. The phone rang, but Nancy, feeling lethargic, remained on the couch. The noise finally stopped but started right back up again.

This time it rang until the answering machine picked up. Nancy sat up when she heard Mrs. Portson's frantic voice. Quickly, she grabbed the phone. "Mrs. Portson, I'm here. What is it? Slow down. Okay. Try to calm down. I'll be right over."

Nancy quickly changed out of her business clothes and into a pair of jeans, a comfortable shirt, and a pair of tennis shoes. She snatched up her purse and ran out of her apartment. Her energy had returned in full force.

The drive to Denten did not seem as long as it usually did. She pulled up next to the big red barn in the back yard of the Portsons' house as Mrs. Portson had instructed her to do. Mrs. Portson was sitting on an old wooden chair inside the barn. Nancy ran up to her. "What did Philip send to you?"

"This," Mrs. Portson said holding the envelope out to Nancy.

Nancy took the envelope that was addressed to the Portsons. She recognized it. It was the envelope that she had written out for Philip at the hospital. Quickly, she removed the papers inside. The first picture was of the red barn that Mrs. Portson and her were inside of. This picture had Nancy in it, and it showed her up on a ladder climbing up to a hayloft. Nancy looked around the barn and spotted a ladder. Nancy looked at the next picture. It was of the inside of the barn again, though this time, there was a large easel set up in it and a huge portrait of Jane Fellow on it. Across from the portrait, sat Jane in the nude. Philip was painting. In the third picture, Jane was gone, and Philip was holding the portrait of Jane that was dripping with blood. The last picture was of an old wooden crate.

"What does this mean, Nancy?"

"I don't know. I'm going up that ladder."

"Be careful."

Nancy slowly went up the ladder. She looked around the hayloft on the upper deck of the barn until she spotted the wooden crate. It was padlocked. She carried it down the ladder.

CHAPTER 16

▼

CONFESSIONS

The following morning, Nancy awoke to the phone ringing. She decided to let her answering machine get it but heard Jack Stenson's voice. Quickly, Nancy stumbled out of bed and ran to the phone. Too late, he'd hung up. His message was about Claudia's newspaper. Normally, she would wait until she made it into work to read a copy, but Jack's voice sounded agitated. She threw on a pair of jeans and a tee shirt and ran down stairs to the newspaper stand just in front of the little store near her apartment building.

The front page of *News To Know* carried the headline "More Evidence In the Philip Secured Case," and half of the page contained a picture of the wooden crate that Nancy had found in the Portsons' barn. Fuming, she skimmed the article. It was continued on the next two pages.

Nancy drove directly to the old building that Claudia had rented out in the crime infested area of the city. She stormed into Claudia's little office and slammed the paper down on her desk. "What is this?"

Claudia smiled. "It looks like my newspaper to me."

"You know what I mean."

"It's a story, an important one that you were planning to hold out on me. I know you, Nancy. When you asked for some time off from covering the trial, I had you followed. I knew you were up to something."

"Up to something? I wanted time off because I was tired, and I needed a break."

"Then how do you explain finding the portrait?"

"You know how. You wrote about it in your paper. Philip drew some pictures. How did you get all this information?"

"The guy that was following you interviewed Mrs. Portson after you left."

"You're disgusting."

"No, I'm smart."

"I quit."

"Good, because I'm being bought out at noon today, and we're all starting back at *The Doverlaine Daily* next week. Oh, and they want you to continue covering the trial. Plus, you're getting a raise."

"I'm quitting this business. It's sneaky. Your friends back stab you."

"You're too sensitive." Claudia waited for Nancy's comeback, but there wasn't one. She looked at her. "Oh, you're not going to cry are you?"

"No."

"You can't give up your job at the paper? What will you do? Oh, I know, you'll live off your parents. I forgot how they pamper you. You pout, and they hand you money. Me, I'm in debt up to my ears from the strike; but you, with your parents' help, you must have floated above it all. While the rest of us have trudged along and struggled through this mess, you've lain back on your raft with a glass of champagne."

"I didn't take any money from them. I'm in debt too, Claudia."

"Oh, don't give me that. You have a way out any time you want it."

"I don't want them supporting me."

"Then, you're not quitting the paper?" Claudia smiled.

Nancy broke down in tears. She was crying hard. Claudia closed her office door. "Nancy, I'm sorry."

"What if those are Philip's fingerprints on that portrait?"

Claudia thought about that implication when she first heard about the portrait of Jane and the bloody fingerprints on it. She guided Nancy to the chair at her desk. "Sit down, Nancy. You can't be responsible for everything."

"Claudia, if those are Philip's fingerprints, look what I've done."

"You've done nothing but try to get to the truth. Suppose those are Philip's fingerprints, then you've found real evidence that he committed the murder. You didn't plant it like Richard and the others. No one will have to worry about an innocent man in prison."

"What will happen to Richard, Dr. Kebler, Chief Randall? Their lives will be destroyed, and it'll be my fault. They'll lose their careers. They'll probably have to serve time in jail, maybe even prison."

"They deserve to. I don't care if they were right about Philip. That doesn't give them the right to plant evidence on him. You said it yourself, Nancy: 'if they get away with planting evidence on Philip, they could do it to anybody: you, me, anybody!'"

Nancy took a tissue from the box and wiped her eyes, then blew her nose. Somehow, Claudia had chipped the guilt away. "Maybe, they're not Philip's fingerprints."

"Let me get you a cup of coffee." Claudia opened her office door and called out for Sally.

Sally wheeled the coffee cart up to Claudia's office door. She looked in at Nancy. "Two cups, Claudia?"

"Yes."

"Nancy, you like cream and sugar with yours, right? Claudia, I know how you take it."

"Yes, you do and it's always delicious. Sally, when we get back to our regular jobs at *The Doverlaine Daily*, I'm going to tell the boss to give you a raise."

Sally strode away with a smile on her face. Nancy took a sip of her coffee. "Claudia, how can you do that to her?"

"What? She deserves a raise. She makes the best coffee I've ever drank in my life."

"This is practically your paper. You're one of the investors, and you didn't let her write one story for you. Next week, you'll be editor in chief of *The Doverlaine Daily* again, and you're going to keep her as the coffee girl. How long are you going to treat her like this?"

"Nancy, you don't understand. She's the best at what she does. I just can't picture someone else getting me my coffee. I like her. I'd miss her smile and her manners. I mean, she's always so polite. She's the only person that's worked for me and has never said anything mean to me."

"Claudia, she's probably holding all of it in. You've covered stories yourself about disgruntled employees. It's always the nice employee that never had a bad word to say about anybody that ends up blowing the boss away."

Claudia burst out laughing as she tried to picture sweet little Sally toting a machine gun into the building. "Oh, you're being silly."

"And you're being mean."

"Fine, I promise, I'll give her a story to write." Claudia took a big sip of her coffee. "It'll be hard, but I'll promote her. Now, get out of my chair and go home and rest. You've got two days, and then you're back to covering that trial."

"Oh, don't, Claudia."

"Don't what?"

"Don't make it sound like you're giving me time off because it's your idea. The court's in a two day recess to examine the new evidence."

"I could always have you cover something else for those two days."

"Fine, Claudia, thank you, your majesty, for the time off." She bowed.

Nancy left Claudia's office wasting no time. She sped along with the flow of rush hour traffic and was soon home resting on her couch.

It wasn't long before she fell into a heavy sleep. Even Clansy who jumped up on her and walked around until he found a place to nestle, did not wake her. She was too busy dreaming to pay any attention to the real world. Philip was sitting in prison reaching out to her and repeating the words, "I'm innocent." She saw Richard on his knees in front of her, "Nancy, you don't know what you're doing. He's guilty." And, out of nowhere, Sally appeared with her coffee cart and a machine gun strapped to her back. Then, the scene changed, and Nancy was looking into the Portsons' red barn. Philip was painting Jane when suddenly, his paintbrush turned into a big ugly knife. He turned and ran at Jane with it. Her eyes widened. She screamed like a police siren. Nancy shot up into a sitting position on the couch. Outside her window, she heard the siren and realized that a police car was traveling down the street and that its siren had found its way into her dream.

The phone was ringing. Nancy wiped the sweat from her forehead and picked up the receiver. She was surprised to hear Helen's voice. "I'm still in town, and I need to talk to you. I'm staying with the Bartons."

Nancy agreed to meet Helen at Ken Barton's store. Without hesitation, she drove to Denten. Often, she looked at her rearview mirror to make sure that no one was following her.

When she arrived at the store, Ken told her that Helen was at the small white church. Nancy remembered seeing it and knew where it was.

It did not take her long to drive there. She stepped into the church and immediately saw Helen.

Helen crossed over to her. "Hello."

Her voice sounded nervous, and she was fidgeting. Nancy knew that whatever she was going to tell her was definitely another piece of the puzzle.

"This is private. Please, promise me that what I say to you will not end up in the newspaper."

"I promise." Nancy looked out the window to see if she would be able to keep that promise. There were no other cars in the parking lot except hers and Helen's. Nancy sat down on one of the long bench seats.

Helen sat in a wooden chair directly across from Nancy. Her voice was shaky. "Nancy, I want you to know that my husband is a good man, and when you have to write about him, I want you to remember that. He didn't mean to kill Jane. It was my fault that he was so jealous. That night, he thought that I was Jane. He'd gone to the barn to find me with Philip. He thought that we were having an affair, and instead, Jane was there."

"You mean, he would have killed you?"

"He was jealous. He warned me to stay away from Philip."

"He would have killed you?"

"It was my fault. I caused him to be jealous. He thought that Jane was me and he…"

"You and Jane look nothing alike."

"It must have been dark in the barn that night."

"Did your husband confess to you that he murdered Jane?"

"No, but I know. I've always known. He did it."

"What proof do you have?"

"He didn't come home that night until after midnight. He had blood on his hands when he came in. I saw him go into the bathroom and wash it off. I asked him if he was hurt, and he said that he cut his hand on a broken test tube. He didn't have any cuts on his hands. I checked in the morning before he woke up. When I noticed that Philip's test tube was missing, he said that it was the one that had broken, but I told him that I knew that wasn't true. There wasn't any broken glass in the trash cans. He told me that he couldn't tell me what was going on, or I would be hurt. He said that what he was doing would protect me."

"Why would killing Jane protect you? Do you think that he killed her to setup Philip? Jane was his cousin's wife. How could he do that?"

"I don't know, but he had blood on his hands. On the stand, he confessed to framing Philip. I just know that those fingerprints on Jane's portrait are going to be his."

Helen was crying, and Nancy knew the right thing to do sociably would be to feel sorry for her, but she could not. Her sympathy was for Philip. Why are you telling me all of this? She thought. It would have helped had you told me this sooner. Jack could have asked certain witnesses the right kind of questions that would have identified your husband as the murderer.

"You knew that he'd committed this murder, but you let Philip go to prison for it. Why?"

"I told you before; I'd never hurt my husband."

"Did he ask you to lie?"

"No. He doesn't know that I know."

"You said that you told him what you knew."

"About the conspiracy to frame Philip, but not that he killed Jane."

"Why are you telling me this?"

"I don't want him hurt."

"He tried to kill you, and you're afraid of him getting hurt?"

Nancy heard a car door shut. She stood up and went to the window. Looking out at the Mercedes, she said, "Speak of the devil."

Helen stood up, fear on her face. "Not Keith!"

"He's coming in. Helen, don't worry. I won't tell him anything."

He barely had a foot in the building when Helen rushed over to him and dramatically draped herself all over him. "I thought you were testifying," she said quickly.

"No. They called for a two day recess so that they can examine some new evidence." He began kissing her passionately everywhere: on her face, her shoulders, her hands. "They have a portrait of Jane with some bloody fingerprints on it."

Helen shot away from him, crying uncontrollably. "Why? Why did you do it?"

He ran to her and held her in a tight embrace. "For you. Helen, I framed Philip for you. Please believe me, Helen. I'd do anything for you. I love you."

Helen pulled away again. "Keith, you're going to go to prison."

"Better me than you, Helen."

Nancy stood stiffly up against the wall watching them. Helen was now flinging herself at her husband's feet and grabbing hold of his legs. "Oh, Keith. Why did you have to kill Jane? I don't understand."

His eyes narrowed as he peered down at her. "What? I didn't kill Jane." He pulled her up and held her by both shoulders.

"You knew how I felt about Philip. You killed Jane so that you could frame Philip, and I would never see him again."

His voice became harsh. "I know how you felt about him. You were so in love with him that you killed Jane. You didn't want him painting her."

"That's not true. I was the one who told her to get her portrait done."

"You must have regretted telling her that because you killed her."

Helen yanked away from him. "I did not; you did."

"No. After work that night, I came home to an empty house, and I knew just where you were. I knew you'd gone to see Philip. I told you that I wanted you to stay away from him, but you went and finished that painting in the Portsons' barn."

"That was weeks before…"

"Before Jane's death. I know. But afterwards, you were still sneaking around the Portsons' place to see Philip."

"I wasn't. I was at the town meeting the night she was murdered. You were the one who came home with blood on your hands."

"Because I was covering your tracks, that's why. I saw Jane running from the barn that night. She was bleeding and screaming. I tried to stop her, but she was delirious. She pulled a knife out of her body. It was your knife, Helen, the one that I bought for you. It had your initials inscribed in it."

"What knife? I don't remember you giving me a knife."

"It had a pink handle. I used to joke with you about our going hunting together. You said that you would never kill a helpless animal, remember? As a joke, I bought that knife for you."

"I gave it away."

"To who?"

"I don't remember. It was years ago. Maybe I gave it to Jane."

"Jane pulled your knife out of her stomach and ran to her car. I followed her trying to catch her. She stopped at a party store in the city, and I was able to get her into my truck."

"A white truck?" Nancy asked.

He looked at her as though she had just materialized. "Yes," he answered now conscientiously aware that he was confessing.

"Helen, I thought that you had stabbed her. It was your knife. I wanted to protect you. When I first got her into my truck, I tried to stop the bleeding. I was driving to the hospital, but she died. That's when I took her to the alley, and I stabbed her body a couple of times to make it look like she'd been attacked by someone crazed. It was so awful."

"That you screamed?" Nancy asked.

He paused for a moment and looked at Nancy. He nodded his head. "I took the knife, and I left her there. I didn't want you going to prison, Helen. I called Richard, and I told him that Philip was dangerous and that he'd better save Jane. He didn't know where she was at. Hours later, someone found her."

"Josephine saw your shadow that night." Nancy was certain now that Josephine only lied about the time and the identity of the person with the knife.

"Richard and Chief Randall came to our house, and I helped them frame Philip. Richard believed that Philip did it."

"I didn't do it, Keith. How could you even think that I could kill?" She passed out and dropped to the floor.

Keith had her in his arms within seconds. "Helen, Helen, I'm sorry."

Nancy stood motionless. The puzzle pieces were coming together and apart at the same time. Neither one of them had confessed to killing Jane, but both had suspected the other.

As Helen reached consciousness, Nancy asked, "Keith, did you touch Jane's portrait?"

He looked at her quizzically. Then, he slowly shook his head no. "I thought that they were Helen's fingerprints. I don't know who's they are."

CHAPTER 17

▼

FINGERPRINTS

The following day, Nancy thanked Sister Roletta for meeting her at the hospital so that she could get in to see Philip. He was watching TV. "Philip, how are you feeling?"

He pulled his covers back and adjusted his bed so the head would rise. He smiled at her. "Better. The doctors told me that the medicine is working." His smile shifted into a frown. "I'll be going back to prison soon."

"Philip, maybe not. You know that your trial is going on. Well, right now it's not because the court is in recess.

"Recess?"

"The lawyers are taking a break to examine new evidence: the portrait I found of Jane. Tell me, Philip, why you didn't mention the portrait in your first trial?"

"No one asked me about it." He was making a great effort to sit up. "I was never allowed to talk."

"But, why didn't you tell the Portsons about it? Philip, why didn't you tell me about it? Don't you trust me?"

"Nancy, I promised Jane that I wouldn't tell anyone. I was trying to keep my promise to her. I drew you the pictures because I do trust you."

"Philip, Jane's gone, and you're the one we have to help. It's okay to tell people about the portrait now. Do you understand?"

He nodded his head. "I want you to help me. I don't want to go back to prison."

"Are the bloody fingerprints on Jane's portrait yours?"

"No."

"Why did you hide the portrait?"

"It was supposed to be a secret. Jane didn't want anyone to know about it."

"Whose fingerprints are on the portrait?"

He shook his head. "I don't know."

"Did you see the fingerprints when you put the painting away?"

"Yes. I saw blood on the ground."

"Why didn't you call the police?"

"I was scared."

"Philip, what happened that night that you were painting Jane in the barn, the night that she was murdered?"

"I went in the barn to paint Jane. We were almost done. I was just going to touch it up some. It was our last time, and she was waiting for me. I went next door 'cause Brian Robbin's dog had puppies, and he said that I could pick mine out. I couldn't have it. He said not until it got bigger. Its eyes were still closed."

"What happened when you returned to the barn?"

"Jane was gone. There was blood in a puddle on the hay where she had been posing and on her portrait and on the ground. There was a trail of blood that went to where her car had been parked."

"Why didn't you tell the Portsons?"

"I told you, the painting was a secret. I didn't know what happened. I was scared."

"What did you do?"

"I cleaned up the blood, and I hid the portrait."

"Did you see anyone else that night besides Brian Robbin?"

"No."

"What about his mother or father? He couldn't have been at home alone."

"There was no one with us at his house. I didn't see anyone there but Brian. Oh, yeah, there were the puppies and their mother. She was nursing them."

"Philip, what did you think happened to Jane?"

"I didn't know."

The door opened. A man wearing a long white coat and carrying a clip-board stepped into the room. "Time for your medicine Philip." He smiled at Nancy. "How are you today, Sister?"

Nancy almost forgot that she was dressed in the habit. "Good, thank you." She smiled.

"Nancy, I wish I knew who touched the painting."

She quickly patted his shoulder. "Don't worry about it, Philip. Just concentrate on getting well."

When Nancy and Sister Roletta walked out of the hospital, Claudia ran up behind them in the parking lot. "So, Sister Nancy, what did you find out?"

Nancy jumped. "Shit, you scared the hell out of me!"

"Sister, should you be cursing like that?" Claudia laughed.

"Claudia, what are you doing here?"

"Trying to make sure that I don't get left out of the latest news."

Nancy introduced Claudia to Sister Roletta as they walked to their cars. "Did you follow me, Claudia?"

"No."

"How did you know that I was here?"

"What did Philip tell you? Did he say that the fingerprints were his?"

"He said that they weren't, and no, he doesn't know whose fingerprints they are."

"What else did he tell you?"

"Nothing else."

"Nancy, are you holding information from me?"

"Claudia, you gave me time off remember. Now, quit following me. If I find anything out, you'll be the first to know."

Sister Roletta got into her car. "Good-bye."

"Thanks again for your help." Nancy waited until the nun drove away, and then she turned to Claudia. "I'm worried."

"About what?"

"What if Philip touched the portrait and forgot that he touched it?"

"He'll be found guilty for sure."

Nancy rubbed her forehead for a second and then pointed her right index finger at Claudia. "It's possible that he didn't kill her but touched the blood and then the portrait."

"Him hiding it in that crate is going to make him look guilty."

"I know," Nancy said sounding tired. She unlocked her car.

"Where are you headed?"

Nancy noticed that Claudia's car was parked near hers. "Home. Will you be stopping by to visit me, or are you going to follow me home and sit out in the parking lot spying on me?"

"I'll do you one better. I'm going to buy you lunch at that Italian restaurant around the corner. They have lobster spaghetti."

"It sounds good as long as you don't ask me anymore questions about Philip." Nancy pulled the habit off revealing her blue jeans and a sweater. She placed the habit in her trunk.

"I promise no questions. We won't even discuss work."

Three bites into her meal, Claudia wanted to know why Nancy had met Helen and her husband at the church. "Didn't think I knew about that, did you?"

Nancy did not even ask Claudia how she found out about the meeting. She simply stood up and left the restaurant. None of Claudia's apologies or pleas worked to change Nancy's mind.

After arriving home, Nancy sat down on her couch, and Clansy curled up on her lap. It comforted her to pet him. Just when she thought that she could relax, the phone rang.

It was Ellen Portson on the line. Ed was disturbed by something and had not eaten all day. Ellen told Nancy that he was refusing to talk to her about what was troubling him. Before Nancy had time to remind herself that she was tired and needed to take a rest, she was promising to drive out to Denten before dark.

Nancy hurried off to the Portsons' house. The drive seemed shorter every time that she drove out there. She had been there so much lately that it was beginning to seem like her second home.

In the kitchen, Mrs. Portson and Nancy ate dinner while Ed just sat there looking worried. Mrs. Portson cleared the table and poured Nancy a cup of coffee. She offered her husband a cup, but he refused.

Nancy whispered into Ellen's ear. "Maybe he'll talk to me."

Ellen's worried face let a slight smile make its way to the surface. She left the two of them in the room and hoped that Nancy could help Ed.

Nancy had no idea what she should say to Mr. Portson or if she should truly say anything at all. She studied his face. He turned away from her. "Mr. Portson, I know it's not any of my business, but your wife is worried about you. She said that you quit eating today and that you won't talk to her. She thinks something is troubling you."

He looked at her. His eyes were watering, and he looked tired. "I read the newspaper about the portrait. The fingerprints, they're mine."

Nancy never expected him to say that. She never suspected him; nobody did. He could hardly get around without his walker.

"I went out to Philip's little house, but he wasn't there. I saw a light on in the barn. I didn't know what he was doing in there. I figured it out awfully quick when I seen the portrait of the naked lady. I saw something wet on the ground, and I touched it. It was blood. I was worried about Philip. I went to look for him. I thought that he was hurt."

"Then what happened?"

"I guess I touched the portrait."

"Mr. Portson, why didn't you say something about this earlier?"

"I didn't think that it would help. I didn't know what had happened to that portrait anyway. There just didn't seem to be a reason to mention it."

Mr. Portson would surely be a murder suspect because his fingerprints were on Jane's portrait. The police, she knew would be coming soon for him. She wasted no time in calling Jack Stenson. "Jack, I know whose fingerprints they are. They're Ed Portsons. He didn't murder Jane. I'm out here right now talking to him. Jack, he's going to need a good lawyer."

CHAPTER 18

▼

CLUE

In the morning, Nancy was in her friend's cramped office. "Claudia, would you please sit down?"

"I have to be out of here in an hour or they'll charge me another day of rent." She swung open the door. "Sally," she hollered down the hall.

Sally soon stood before her.

"Make sure everyone has packed everything up and nobody leaves anything behind. Get Jimmy for me too; will you please?"

Within seconds Jimmy was standing before Claudia.

"Is the truck loaded up? I don't want any of those computers left behind."

"Hello, Nancy, how are you? Your coverage has been great." He smiled.

Claudia put her hands on her hips. "Jimmy, what about the truck?"

"It's loaded up."

"The computers?"

"They're all on the truck." He smiled at Nancy again. "I haven't seen you, not since our date. I know you've been busy, but maybe we could have dinner?"

Nancy shifted in her seat. "Well, I…"

"Jimmy, go finish your work. Ask her out to dinner on your own time."

"Claudia, it was my money that got you where you are."

"Jimmy, I'm standing inside of a filthy, ought to be condemned building in the center of a crime ridden neighborhood, and I get paid peanut shells. Do you really think that your statement is appropriate?"

"Beggars shouldn't be choosy."

"Jimmy, if you want some of your investment back, I suggest that you make sure those computers are packaged well. The company that's buying them made it clear that they won't pay for any damaged ones. Don't forget this desk and chair. They'll be out in the hall in a few minutes."

Jimmy smiled once again at Nancy. "I'll see you later, sweety," he promised her before leaving.

Nancy felt a headache beginning. "Claudia, did you hear anything that I've said?"

"Yes, I was listening. You believe everyone's story and no one did it, which means, you want to believe that everyone is innocent and no one is a liar."

"I didn't say that. I said…"

"I know what you said. And, I also know that you are gullible."

Nancy stood up and pushed the chair up to the desk. "I came here because I thought that you might be able to help me."

"With what? You should be at home on your laptop writing about everything that you've told me. It's tomorrow's headlines on the front page, and you're hanging out in my office." Claudia propped the door open with a rubber doorstop. She pulled her desk forward. Nancy pulled the chair away and shoved the desk towards Claudia. Together they moved the desk into the hall. Nancy shoved the chair out the door too. They both returned to the office. Claudia began filling the large cardboard box with papers and other supplies.

"Claudia, I don't think any of them are lying."

"My point exactly. You like to believe that everyone is honest."

"Claudia, you're impossible." Nancy headed out of the office.

"Nancy, the head honcho wants to see you in his office tomorrow morning at nine o'clock."

"Why?"

"I don't know. I told you before, he wants you to keep covering the trial."

"No doubt."

"Maybe, he wants to see you, Nancy, so that he can ask you how your father's doing. Maybe, he just wants to check up on his golfing buddy."

"Knock it off, Claudia." Nancy stepped into the hallway and closed the door.

"What? What did I say?" Claudia yelled after her.

Nancy went straight home to think about everything. She paced back and forth in her living room. Philip had to be the one that stabbed Jane if Mr. Portson didn't. Why would he stab her and then leave to look at the Robbins' puppies? Philip said that Brian Robbin told him that he could come and pick out a puppy. There's no phone out in the barn. Brian Robbin must have told Philip in person about the puppies that very night, before Jane was murdered. Excited about choosing a puppy, Philip drops what he's doing and leaves his company waiting in the barn. That's it: Brian Robbin must have seen Jane in the barn when he spoke to Philip. He may have seen what happened to her, or maybe he heard people talking, her screaming, or some kind of noise.

Nancy dreaded the long drive to Denten, but tomorrow, court would be in session again, and she would be back to work covering the trial. She would have to leave right now if she wanted to get there during the afternoon.

CHAPTER 19

▼

BRIAN ROBBIN

Nancy turned her car into the Robbins' driveway. The seven-year-old boy with the thick brown hair and the big blue eyes was in the front yard throwing a baseball into the air and catching it with his glove. She recognized him as the boy who she had seen in Ken Barton's store.

Not wanting to frighten him, Nancy asked to speak to one of his parents. He took a long look at her. "They're not home."

"Oh. Do you know when they'll be back?"

"No."

Nancy wondered how his parents could leave him home all alone when he was so young. "I'm a friend of Ed and Ellen Portson, your next door neighbors. I'm also a friend of Philip's. He told me that you had a puppy for him. I thought, maybe, your parents could show it to me. That way I can tell Philip how his puppy is doing."

"I can show it to you."

It didn't feel right to ask him questions without having his parents' permission, but Nancy swallowed her guilt and fired away.

"Do you remember the night that Philip came over to your house to see your puppies?"

"Yes," he replied looking up at her.

"Were you at the barn that night to get Philip?"

He looked away from Nancy and nodded his head.

"Did you talk to Philip?"

He looked down at his shoes. "Yes."

Brian said nothing for a few seconds and then he quickly blurted out, "I was there twice."

"Twice?"

"Yes, Ma'am."

Nancy bent down and looked into Brian's face. His ears had suddenly turned red. "Why were you there twice?"

"To tell Philip about the puppies being born."

"Why twice?"

"The first time, he was busy."

"Busy with what?"

"Painting."

"You saw him painting?"

He stared down at his shoes. With a frown on his face, he answered yes.

"Did you see the woman that Philip was painting?"

His small face turned red, and he merely nodded his head.

She realized now why he seemed so embarrassed. He had seen Jane's naked body.

"Did Philip tell you to go away because he was busy?"

"No, my daddy told me to go home."

"Your dad was there?"

The boy nodded his head.

"So, you didn't talk to Philip because your dad told you to go home?"

He nodded his head.

"The first time you went to the barn, you saw Philip and the woman that he was painting, but you didn't talk to Philip. Is that right?"

Once again the boy turned red and again nodded his head.

"Did Philip let you in?"

"No."

Nancy was confused. "Well, how did you see Philip painting if you weren't in the barn?"

He focused his eyes on his shoes. When he finally looked up, he looked past Nancy and yelled out, "Mom, did you get me ice cream?"

Nancy watched Brian run to his mom as she walked into the yard carrying a small sack of groceries. Mrs. Robbin had dark brown hair that was pulled back into a bun behind her head. She was tall with a thick body.

Lowering the grocery bag so that her son could see the box of chocolate ice cream, she smiled. "Yes, I have your treat. Now, you go and get washed up."

Nancy walked up to her. "Hello, I'm Nancy Mead. I'm a friend of the Portsons. I'm also a friend of Philip Secured. I hope that you don't mind, but I was just visiting next door, and I saw your son. He was going to show me the dog that you saved for Philip. That certainly was a nice thing for you and your family to do for Philip."

"I know who you are. Everyone in town does. We're all glad that you're helping Philip." She smiled. "Look, follow me into the house. I'll get these groceries put away, and we can have a glass of ice tea."

"Okay. Thank you."

Nancy didn't know how to just come out and ask Mrs. Robbin the questions that she needed to have answered, but she knew that she had to do it. Nancy took a big gulp of her tea. "Thank you for the ice tea. You make it just as delicious as Mrs. Portson."

"Oh, now that's a big compliment. I just love Ellen's tea. She's the best when it comes to fixing ice tea or cooking."

"You're right. She's a terrific cook. I'm having lunch with her in about an hour."

"Oh, I should start making lunch. Brian always comes home for it."

Just then, Brian came running into the kitchen. "I'm all clean. Can I have my ice cream?"

"You can wait until after lunch."

"Mom, please, I want some now."

"No. You'll wait until your father gets home. We'll all have lunch together, and then you can have a bowl of ice cream."

"Mom," he whined.

"You bug me anymore about it, you won't get any. Go on and feed the dogs."

"Your husband's name is Brian too?" Nancy asked.

"Right."

"I was wondering if you and your husband wouldn't mind answering a few questions for me?"

She smiled enthusiastically, her eyes lighting up. "Are my answers going to be put into the paper like the Portsons' and the Bartons' were?"

"Maybe."

"Well, I don't mind answering any questions, but my husband, I can't say. He turns off the TV whenever any news coverage about the trial comes on. If it's on the front cover of the newspaper, he throws it away without even reading one word. He cannot stand to hear anyone talking about Jane Fellow, good or bad."

"Why is that?"

"I'm not sure."

"Did he know Jane Fellow?"

"Everybody knew her. This is a small town. Everyone knows everyone here. Even strangers aren't strangers for very long. That's why when I seen you talking to my boy, it didn't bother me. You've been around this town enough that a lot of people know you."

"I have been in town a lot." Nancy smiled. "Um, I was wondering Mrs. Robbin what you thought of Jane Fellow?"

"She was a nice person. When her and her husband would come to visit Dr. Kebler and Helen, Jane would attend church with Helen. Sometimes her children played with Brian. Jane was a nice person, very friendly. She really admired that husband of hers. She was proud of his being a mayor."

Brian ran into the kitchen and sat in the chair next to Nancy. "I'm done feeding the dogs. Philip's dog eats the most."

"Does he?" Nancy smiled at Brian. "What is his name?"

"He doesn't have one. My mom said that Philip gets to name him because it's his dog. So, I just call him dog. My dog's name is Sprite. When I spilled my pop one time, he drank it all up off the floor."

Nancy turned her attention back to Brian's mother. "Did your husband like Jane?"

"No." Mrs. Robbin covered her mouth and leaned towards Nancy's ear. She whispered into it, "He thought she was a slut."

Brian looked at his mother quizzically.

"Why?" Nancy asked.

"Brian, go out and play with your dogs, honey."

"But I just got cleaned up."

"Go play."

He left the room, and Mrs. Robbin explained to Nancy, "Well, he thought that she was a bad influence on the women in this town."

"Why?"

"Something about her morals or lack of."

"What did he know about her?"

"He just hated her. I don't know why, but he just was so mad at her one night. In fact, it was the night that she was murdered. He'd been complaining about what a slut she was, and I remember telling him to stop talking that way because I didn't want Brian Jr. to pick up that kind of language."

"You were home that night?"

"No, I went to the town meeting, but I talked with Brian after I got home."

Nancy took a big swallow of her ice tea. "Anybody in your family own a hunting knife with a pink handle?"

"How did you know about that? Don't say anything to Brian Jr. about it. Philip gave him one, but he can't have it until he gets older. I put it up for him. His dad doesn't want him to have it because he says that the pink handle will make him a sissy. Brian just loves Philip, and since Philip gave him that knife, he's Brian's best friend. Brian is always strapping the thing to his belt and sneaking out of the house with it. I've put it up on the highest shelf in the cabinet to keep him from finding it."

"Helen Kebler said that she gave her hunting knife to someone. It must have been to Philip, and then he gave it to your son."

Mrs. Robbin seemed to be thinking about something. "Oh, that must be why the knife has H. K. on it, for Helen Kebler."

"Do you have the knife?"

"Sure, it's up in the cabinet."

"May I see it?"

Mrs. Robbin reached up and opened the door to the cabinet that was above the stove, and she searched for the knife. "Brian!" she hollered. Mrs. Robbin put her hands on her hips waiting for her son to enter the kitchen. Letting out a heavy sigh, she looked him in the eyes. Sternly, she asked, "Young man, where is that hunting knife?"

"Mom, I don't know."

"Yes, you do."

"No, Mom, I don't."

"Well, it's not where I hid it. And, if you don't tell me what you did with it, I'm going to have a talk with your father about it when he gets home."

"Daddy caught me with it and took it away."

Brian left the kitchen with his head hung low and his shoulders sagging. Nancy saw the last puzzle piece go into place. "Mrs. Robbin…."

"Please, call me Ireen."

"Ireen, Philip said that he came over here on the night that Jane was murdered to look at your puppies. He said that no one but your son was in the house."

"That's impossible because my husband was here watching Brian. I never leave my boy home alone unless I'm just running up to the store for a few things, like I just did today."

"Was he here when you came home that night?"

"Yes, of course, in fact, he was doing my choirs for me. I remember 'cause he hardly ever does that. I'm not complaining mind you 'cause I never do his either."

"What was he doing?"

"Washing clothes." She began laughing. "I was pleased, but at the same time, I was hoping he wasn't shrinking or dyeing anything."

Nancy smiled trying to seem amused, but she was sick knowing that he had ruined more than clothing.

Suddenly, Ireen leaned out the doorway of the kitchen. "You hear that?"

"What?" Nancy asked.

"It sounds like," she paused for a second. "Cartoons!"

Nancy right away detected the irritation in Ireen's voice.

"I told him that he is not allowed to watch those violent shows. Excuse me. I'll be right back."

Nancy could hear her yelling at Brian Jr. Ireen's view was strong. Cartoons were nothing more than violent images used to brainwash the young into violent actions. She returned to the kitchen almost out of breath. "I'm sorry about that, but he knows better. I'm the president of PAVS, People Against Violent Shows. I of all people cannot have my child watching any violence."

"I see."

"I send letters and petitions to the television networks and movie producers." She spoke excitedly. "Not just me, but all of the members; there's nine of us. We tape the shows, and we write reports about their level of violence. Right now, we are working on cartoons. We were supposed to do cartoons last year sometime, but most of the members wanted to start with the violent R rated movies first, then the PG-13's and so forth."

"Oh."

"My son had so many cartoon tapes that no one else had to tape any. I feel bad knowing that I let him become exposed to so much violence."

Nancy looked at her watch.

"I'm sorry, Nancy, I didn't mean to go on and on about this."

The front door banged shut. "That's Brian, he's home. Brian, honey, we're in here, in the kitchen," she yelled out. Both Brians entered the kitchen. "I was talking to your father."

Mr. Robbin looked surprised to see Nancy sitting at the table with his wife. He was a tall, heavyset man with thick jet-black hair and blue eyes. He and his blue overalls were covered in grease and dirt. "I have some work to do," he mumbled to Ireen and strode off.

"Wait, honey," she called after him. She ran to talk to him. Nancy could hear them in the other room. "Honey, don't you know who she is? She's Nancy Mead. She's a friend of the Portsons. She's also that reporter. Remember that newspaper I showed you? Well, that's the Nancy that I've been talking about. She's been helping Philip. She wants to ask you some questions."

"Why?"

"She's going to put our names in the paper. You know and have us say something nice about Philip. Just like she did with the Portsons and the Bartsons."

"I don't want to be in the paper, and I don't want you in that paper either. You get rid of her."

"Brian!"

"I mean it."

Nancy heard how harsh his voice sounded, and it scared her. There was no doubt in her mind that he had something to do with Jane's death.

When Mrs. Robbin returned to the kitchen, she looked embarrassed. "I'm sorry about my husband. I guess he's in a bad mood."

"Oh, that's okay. Everyone has a bad day now and then," Nancy said trying to sound relaxed. She held out her arm and looked at her watch so that Irene would notice. "Oh, I better get going. Ellen's probably finished making lunch and is waiting for me." She stood up and walked quickly to the door. "It was nice meeting you."

She drove back over to the Portsons' house. Ellen had just finished fixing lunch. Nancy sat down at the table. "Sorry about not being on time, but Irene sure can talk."

Ellen didn't seem to hear her. "Ed's going to miss his lunch. He always eats lunch at this time."

"Don't worry; they'll feed him." Nancy felt sorry for her elderly friend.

Ellen was definitely miserable without her husband. She took two bites of her sandwich and set it down. Noticeably, she stared at Ed's empty chair.

"He'll be back home before you know it. The police are only questioning him. They haven't charged him with a crime."

"They took Philip in for questioning too, and he never came back."

Nancy didn't know what to reply to her statement. She swallowed her bite of turkey sandwich too soon, and it lodged in her throat. Choking, she quickly gulped down some water.

After dislodging the food, she realized that Ellen hadn't even noticed that she was choking. The elderly woman was helplessly trapped in her own sadness, and her world was narrowed to the feelings of loss and worry.

"Why don't we go out on the front porch and sit on the swing? A little air might do us some good." Nancy stood up and waited for Ellen to join her.

The two women went out to the front porch and sat on the swing. "Nancy, will you stay the night?"

"I wish that I could, but I have a meeting tomorrow with my boss at nine o'clock. Did I tell you that *The Doverlain Daily* is hiring everyone back to work?"

"No."

"It's the newspaper company that I used to work for. Well, anyway, I have a meeting, and afterwards, I have to go to court to cover the trial." Nancy wanted to tell her about Brian Robbin but thought that the shocking news about her next door neighbor would be too upsetting for Mrs. Portson's nerves.

It was a windy and cloudy day. Weather reporters on TV and the radio had forcast thundershowers for the area. Ellen rocked slowly on the swing and didn't even notice the sudden change in the weather.

Nancy observed her friend's distraught face. "Don't worry, Ellen, Ed will be all right. The truth will come out."

The phone rang. Ellen leaped to her feet. "Maybe it's Ed." She hurried back inside. Nancy followed her. "Yes, she's still here. Hello. Hello. That's strange." She hung the phone back up.

"Who was it?" Nancy asked.

"I don't know. It was a man's voice. He asked if you were here."

"Oh, maybe, it was Jack. He knows that I like visiting you. His cell phone probably ran out of power. That happens to me all of the time. I'll call him back later."

Nancy offered to do the dishes. She begged Mrs. Portson to go to her bedroom and lie down for a nap.

Finally, Mrs. Portson agreed and went to her bedroom. While washing dishes, Nancy phoned Jack. The storm was beginning. Looking out the window, she saw that the sky was suddenly dark. The wind had picked up speed and was tossing small objects around the yard, mostly sticks.

Hearing Jack's voice, her attention went from the storm to the phone. "How's Mr. Portson doing? His wife is worried sick. Jack, I've got to talk to you about…. No, don't put me on hold. Jack? Jack? Jack? Oh!"

His voice returned after two minutes. Nancy was washing the dishes with the receiver tucked between her ear and her right shoulder. She was getting a kink in her neck. "Jack, you are so rude. You hang up on Mrs. Portson. You leave me on hold forever. You didn't? You didn't call to find out if I was here? Oh, well, anyway, Jack, I know who murdered Jane." Thunder cracked loudly and lightening lit up the sky. "Jack it was…Jack? Jack?" There was nothing but silence on the other end; the line was dead.

Nancy ran out to her car and brought her cellular phone into the house. Jack could wait. There was no telling how strong her battery was. Quickly, she searched Mrs. Portson's phone book and then telephoned the Sheriff's station. "Sheriff Clifford, this is Nancy. I know who murdered Jane Fellow. It was...." The phone beeped. The low battery light came on. "It was..." The phone beeped again.

"Nancy, who was it? Speak up. There's a lot of static on my end."

"Brian Robbin."

"Who?"

"Brian Robbin."

"I think our connection is about to go. I can't hear you. Are you out at the Portsons'?"

The battery went dead. Mrs. Portson entered the kitchen. "Nancy, did you call me?"

Nancy turned to see Mrs. Portson standing behind her. She looked so fragile and weak. "I'm sorry. I didn't mean to wake you."

"I was awake from the thunder. I thought you called me."

"I was on the phone and the connection was bad. I was shouting, but it didn't help. The phone is dead now."

"Oh, now Ed won't be able to call me. I hope he's all right." She lowered herself into a chair at the table.

Nancy could see that she was crying. "Oh, Mrs. Portson, he'll be fine. I know that he didn't do anything wrong."

"Philip didn't either, and they locked him up."

That was true, so there was nothing that she could say in the defense of the justice system. Again, she wanted to tell her what she had found out about Brian Robbin, but she wasn't sure how Mrs. Portson would take hearing such awful news. Nancy hugged her instead and let her cry on her shoulder.

Once that Mrs. Portson had gone back to bed, Nancy thought of contacting the sheriff again. She knew that she needed only to plug her cell phone into the auxiliary power source in her car in order to use it right away.

The rain was pounding the ground when Nancy sprinted to her car. After searching in the glove box, she found the cord and plugged it into her phone and into her auxiliary power outlet. It would have been perfect had she remembered Sheriff Clifford's phone number. Even though Denten was a small town, it should still have 911 she thought, but it didn't.

Suddenly, there was a loud bang noise, and something had struck the car. She had heard thunder earlier, but this was different. Another bang sounded. That sounds like gunshots she thought. In the rear-view mirror, she saw Brian Robbin running towards her car with a flashlight in one hand and a handgun in the other.

Frantically, her hands searched the dashboard, the seat, and the floor. "My keys? Where? Oh, God! In the house." She jumped out of her car and took off running. Not able to make it inside the house, she ran around the back of it, past the barn, past Philip's little garage-house, and out into the woods.

CHAPTER 20

▼

PRISONER

Nancy ran, dodging tree limbs, slipping in wet grass, and falling down. The ground was mucky so that she lost one tennis shoe. The mud sucked it right off her foot. It was dark, windy, and wet. She could feel the coldness cutting through her skin as she leaned against the large oak tree, panting, trying to catch her breath, and at the same time resting her legs. Nancy listened to the whistling wind and the crackling thunder, and the sound of her own quick heavy breathing. Even her heart pounding had a piece in this orchestra. A more frightening noise emerged, the one that she was solely focused on, the sound of branches crunching under Brian's big heavy boots.

Needing to hide and having nowhere to go led her up a tree. Slowly, she pulled herself up onto that first branch. Steadying herself, she moved onto the next branch. The branches were soaking wet. Slipping and falling were easy things to do. Five branches up, she balanced her feet on a thick branch, and with both hands she gripped tightly onto a branch just above her head.

Lightening hit a tree in the distance and lit up a huge area of the woods. Nancy realized how dangerous her hiding place was, but Brian was near her. She heard him but could not see him. Suddenly, a squirrel jumped from a tree nearby and landed on top of her hands. She panicked, screamed, and yanked her hands up into the air losing her balance. The squirrel leaped away. Nancy continued to fall. Just like a nightmare, down she plummeted, finding each branch with her back. Unlike a dream, she was certain to hit the ground.

"I've got you," the rough voice sounded. It wasn't a reassuring tone used to make her feel safe. It was the tone of a game winner when he knew he had won. Screaming, yelling, fighting, kicking, clawing all failed her. She settled on fainting, but her body would not comply. Nancy was consciously heading into Brian's arms, and there was nothing she could do to stop herself. A gasp of frightened emotion let itself out as she felt his arms catching her. She could hardly breathe as he tightened his hold on her. Her thoughts were running rampant. Where is his gun? If he wants me dead, why did he catch me? Why not just let me fall and then shoot me? Why did he kill Jane? Is he going to kill me too?

Lightning struck nearby, and now, she could see him. She looked up into his hard-featured face and knew that she had to somehow get free if she was going to live. Wiggling hard, her foot with the shoe on it, found its way to his groin. The kick wasn't strong enough to do any damage.

"Stop." He tightened his grip on her. "Stop!"

Nancy quit struggling. She was on the verge of passing out. Her inner voice emerged. Outwit him, it ordered. All at once, she relaxed, and he loosened his hold on her so that she could breathe without rasping.

He pushed, pulled, and tugged her to make her walk with him, forcing her onto his property. Brian shoved her up to a small building and through a small door. He turned on a little battery lamp.

Nancy could see that they were inside of Brian Junior's playhouse. In the center of the tiny room was a small table with two small chairs. In one corner, there was a plastic sink, a plastic phone, and even a plastic refrigerator. Surely, he wouldn't kill me in his son's playhouse.

After forcing her to sit in one of the little chairs, he sat down in the other. He looked awkward in it. Brian cleared his voice and then spit on the floor. "I'm going to tell you what happened."

Nancy just stared at him. She was frightened by his words. *If he tells me, does he have to kill me? Oh God, I don't want to die. Please, don't tell me. Please, don't. Please, don't. Please, don't. Please, don't. Please, don't. Please…*

He let out a heavy sigh and stared down at his black rubbery boots. While he took those moments to collect his words, Nancy concentrated on how to escape. She was free from his grip, but his body was blocking the doorway.

"I was looking for Brian that night. He'd gone out to play, and he hadn't come home." His voice sounded tired and somewhat gentle. "I caught him down at the Portsons' place." A heavy sigh escaped him. "He was peeking through a hole in their barn. I was going to give him a whipping, teach him not to spy, but when I saw what he was seeing…. She was wearing a thin lacey thing. You could see right through it." His voice turned harsh. "Jane was just lying there, sprawled out on a rug that was over the top of a couple stacks of straw. I couldn't believe it," he yelled. "Jane lying there sinning like that. Letting Philip look at her. I told Brian to get home. He started crying, and I took him home." A silence followed.

First, you're going to tell me everything, a big confession, and then you're going to do away with me so that I can never tell anyone else what you've told me. Why tell me? Why waste your time? Will it make you feel better to tell me that you killed her? Will my dying with your ugly secret help you? Please, don't tell me anymore. I don't want to die. Please, don't tell me anymore.

His voice was gentle again. "We stayed home awhile."

Nancy, despite her fear to hear more, she leaned towards him waiting for his next word. Then, what happened? What did you do? She needed to know.

His face reddened, and he jumped up from the little chair knocking it over. Automatically, Nancy kicked at the floor and shoved her seat backwards. Brian angrily slammed his right fist down on the little table causing the weak legs to fold and bring the tabletop crashing to the floor.

"She had no right to let him look at her," he shouted. "He's an idiot, can't even tie his shoe. I'd heard people saying Helen did it too. I didn't believe them, but after seeing Jane, I knew they'd been telling the truth. Jane and Helen were a bunch of damn sinners!"

The doorway was unblocked. Run. Go. Move! Her brain was screaming orders, but her body remained cringing in the chair. Fearfully, she watched Brian slam his fist around, stomp his feet, and shout about who needed to pay for their sins. He rambled relentlessly.

"Helen had everyone thinking she was an angel, always at the church, helping people out, and all the while she'd been fooling around with Philip. That Philip, he may be stupid, but he's a good boy. They were ruining him. I was going to prove it. I was going to show everyone what Jane was really like. She wasn't respectable. No, she wasn't." He shook his head. "No." Brian moved back in front of the doorway, once again blocking her escape route.

For a moment, he was silent. The little lamp's dim light was just enough to make his figure monstrously large and shadowy.

"I," he began speaking slowly, "had Brian go back to the barn and ask Philip to come to our house and pick out his puppy. I was just going to tape her. I wasn't going to hurt her. Just tape her. That's all. When Philip left the barn, I went in with my video camera. I was taping her." His voice grew excited and he began talking faster. "Boy, was she screaming. Trying to get her clothes back on. I told her, I was going to show the tape to the whole town and to everyone in the city where her husband was the mayor." He was laughing. "Oh, yes, I told her everyone would know how she really was and Helen too. She was yelling at me. Calling me crazy. No. No. She was the crazy one, and I was going to prove it. But, then…. She…she…." Brian stopped talking. He walked straight over to Nancy and leaned down putting his face square with hers. "I…didn't touch her. I didn't."

Nancy had sucked in a big breath when she saw him heading at her. It was now caught in her stomach and chest. She could not exhale.

Brian abruptly walked away from her and returned to the doorway. "I tried to help her. She wouldn't let me touch her."

He did not say anything for about ten minutes and then he began talking softly, crying as he did. "I had Brian's knife in my back pocket and…. I'd taken it away from him that night. He's not supposed to have it 'till he gets older. He was never really going to have it. I was going to buy him a better one than that." He suddenly started to laugh softly. "It had a pink handle. Now, that's a girl's knife. My boy wasn't gonna carry nothing sissy like that."

Brian paused for another couple of minutes. Each one seemed like hours to Nancy. He cleared his voice. "Somehow Jane got a hold of that knife. It must have fell out of my pocket. She was pointing it at me. Threatening to kill me. I was laughing at her. I had enough evidence to show people what she was like. I went to leave, but she fell. She tripped on a stack of straw, and I saw her fall on the knife. It went right into her stomach. I tried to help her, but she screamed at me to get away from her. I heard someone coming, and I left. I knew they'd think I did that to her. I ran home. I didn't think she'd die. I didn't. I thought whoever was coming was gonna help her. You know, take her to the doctor. Next day, I heard she was dead from a lot of stab wounds. I couldn't say anything. Everyone would think I did it. Then, I heard like everyone else that Philip did it. I knew there was no way he could've drove to the city, but who was I gonna tell that to?"

He was crying loudly and leaning up against the wall near the doorway. Nancy hoped that he was telling her the truth. "Brian...um....Brian, maybe, if you gave the tape to the police, they could see that you didn't do it."

Brian walked slowly over to her. "I can't find it. I looked everywhere. I don't know what happened to it. I thought I should keep it, you know, incase someone ever thought I did it. I remember putting it on top of the refrigerator. I think my wife threw it out. She'd been throwing away a lot of our tapes around that time."

"Have you asked her about the tape?"

"I can't ask her about that tape."

"Your wife doesn't know about the content of the tape. She wouldn't get suspicious. Brian, I could even ask her. I could tell her that I'm interested in joining her organization. I could find out where she put that tape."

"No. You aren't talking to her at all." He put his right hand into his pocket and gripped an object that Nancy knew was that gun that he had fired earlier.

CHAPTER 21

▼

MISSING

Claudia was seated in a comfortable leather chair behind a large luxurious desk in her spacious office inside the building that produced *The Doverlain Daily*. A police officer was seated in a chair next to the wall across from her, and Jack Stenson was standing in front of her desk. "Jack, she missed her meeting with the head honcho." Claudia was practically yelling at him.

He rubbed his chin. "The sheriff in Denten said that she had phoned him. She had told us both the same thing before she was cut off."

"Which was?"

"I'm not sure I should say at this point."

"At this point?" Claudia yelled. "At this point she is missing. Her car's at the Portsons' place and she isn't. Jack, if you're going to think out loud, you better tell me what's going on."

"Calm down."

"Calm down?" Claudia shot up out of her chair and got up in his face. "Calm down? No, no, no. You, get excited. Get out there and find her."

"I'm a lawyer, not a detective," he shouted back at her. He saw the worried look in her eyes. "Claudia, I 'm worried about her too." He looked at the clock on the wall and then at his watch. "I have to go to the courthouse." Jack looked to the police officer. "Let me know as soon as you find her."

He stood up. "I definitely will."

Claudia watched Jack Stenson leave her office. She sat back down in her chair, but she could not control the nervous energy that she felt. Once again, she was standing and this time she was in the police officer's face. "You're the law, go find her." She watched him quickly place a hand on his gun. "What are doing?" she yelled.

"I'm…I'm….I'm done questioning you." As he was about to leave, his coworker entered, rushed past him, and ran up to Claudia.

"I came as soon as I could, Claudia."

"Oh, Jessie, I'm glad you're here. My friend is missing. Nancy was in Denten last night, and she hasn't returned. She missed her meeting at nine o'clock. She's supposed to be covering the trial. I don't know where she's at."

Jessie hugged her. "Don't you worry, Claudia; I'll find her."

Claudia looked accusingly at the other police officer. "He knows something, and he won't tell me." She turned back to her boyfriend. "Please, Jessie, I need to know if she's in trouble."

"Tell her what you know, Dwayne."

"You know that I'm not supposed to."

"I know a lot of things, Dwayne, like you leaving your shift early yesterday."

"My daughter had a dental appointment."

"In a bowling alley?"

"It was a tournament."

"You didn't have authorization to leave early."

Dwayne frowned but told all that he knew which was only that Nancy had phoned Jack Stenson and Sheriff Clifford telling them both that she knew who killed Jane Fellow. Further, she never said who the murderer was because both times her phone had lost power.

Claudia threatened to look for Nancy alone if Jessie did not take her with him. When he agreed to take her along, Dwayne shook his head and looked the other way.

"Claudia, what about your job?" Jessie asked.

Her first day back to *The Doverlaine Daily* and she was stepping out the door. Quickly, she put her assistant in charge and then buzzed for Sally.

Sally was in her office within seconds and with her coffee cart. She looked at the two officers and then turned to her. "Three coffees, Claudia?"

"No, Sally. I need you to go to the courthouse today and cover the trial."

"Cover the trial?" She looked surprised.

"Yes. Do the paper proud, Sally."

Sally suddenly clutched at the railing on the coffee cart. "But, Claudia, I can't."

Claudia had her boyfriend and Dwayne step out of her office. She had Sally sit down in the seat across from her desk. "Sally, you can do this."

"I don't know, Claudia. I don't think I can. I mean, I haven't covered anything real, just the weather one time and that didn't even get printed."

Claudia knew this was her fault. She also knew now why Sally had turned down Richard's offer to write his book. It wasn't that the money was too low, it was her confidence level. "Oh, no, Sally. You can't do this to me. Nancy's missing, and I've got to go find her. You have to do this. You have to cover that court case. I could put someone else on it, but I'm sure they wouldn't do as good of a job as you."

"Really, Claudia? I don't know. Maybe you should put someone else on it."

"Are you questioning my ability to do my job?"

"Oh, no, Claudia, no….I'm just…."

"Sally, I'll have you know that I'm the best at what I do, and when I choose someone to cover a story, it's because I know that person is right for the job. Now, we are done talking about this. When I return to my office, I better have your story on my desk." She looked sternly at Sally.

Sally swallowed. "You will, Claudia. I'll go to the courthouse right now." She rushed out of the office nearly tripping on the coffee cart.

CHAPTER 22

▼

CLAUDIA

Inside the store, Claudia stood next to Ken Barton as he was answering Jessie's questions. Ken rubbed his chin "Well now, I didn't hear about her being out this way until she'd come up missing. Sheriff Clifford told me that Ellen Portson phoned him this morning. That's when the phones were working again. That's when Ellen told him that she was missing. She said that Nancy helped her into bed that night, and that was the last time she'd seen her. Poor woman, she's a mess. Her husband's been arrested, and now Nancy is missing. She is in no shape to be questioned. I hope you're not thinking about visiting her." He raised his eyebrows to Claudia causing his glasses to rise up a bit on his nose.

"No, of course not," Claudia answered.

"My wife's staying with her for now."

Claudia was disappointed. Her and Jessie returned to the police car. "It doesn't make sense that he didn't know she was in town. She would have driven past his store on the way to the Portsons' house."

"He could have been busy."

"She usually stops in to say hi to him."

"A storm was on its way."

Jessie drove into the Robbins' driveway and parked his car. He got out and so did Claudia. They took turns knocking on the door. "I don't think they're home," Jessie commented.

"I saw the curtain move when we were on our way up here. They're home."

"Well, they're not answering. Come on let's go. We can come back later."

"No, we're here now. These people are obstructing the law; break the door down or something."

"No."

"At least yell, 'this is the police' or I will."

He shook his head slightly. She frowned at him. "Oh, all right." He pounded on the door, "Open up. This is the police."

Nothing happened. Claudia looked disappointed.

"Yell open up again," she demanded.

"Open up," he yelled.

"Or we're breaking down your door," she threatened.

"Claudia, you can't say that."

"Why not?"

"I'll get fired, that's why."

The door opened. Brian Robbin mustered a smile. "Hello, officer."

"We have some questions to ask you," Claudia said.

Jessie turned to Claudia. "Let me handle this." He cleared his voice. "I have some questions to ask you."

"Yeah, okay."

"May we come in?" Jessie said reaching for his hat on the top of his head.

"No."

Jessie quickly removed his hand leaving his hat on. Claudia peered at Brian. "Why not?" she asked.

"My wife just shampooed our carpet and mopped our floors."

Jessie nodded his head. "I understand. Are you Brian Robbin?"

"Yes, Sir."

"Did you know Nancy Mead?"

"Heard of her."

"You never met her?"

"No."

"The reason we're here is because she is missing. She was last seen next door by Mrs. Portson last night during the storm. Did you see her at all yesterday?"

"No."

"Okay, well if you hear or see anything that might help us find her, give me a call. Here's my number," he said holding out a business card to Brian.

Claudia put her foot in the doorway. "Hold on, what about your wife? Is she home? Maybe she saw Nancy."

"She's not home."

"You just said that she cleaned the carpet and the floors."

"She did. Then, she went to the store."

"We were just at the store. We didn't see her."

"She's still walking to it.'

"We didn't see her on the road."

"She takes a short cut through the woods." He pulled on his door once more to close it. Reluctantly, Claudia removed her foot.

On their way back to the police car, Jessie turned to her. "Claudia, if you do that again, I'm going to make you wait in the car."

"He looks guilty."

"You can't tell if he's guilty."

"Yes, I can. I'm very good at reading people, and he knows something. I say we go back and search his house."

"We don't have a search warrant."

"Let's get one."

"It's not that easy. I have to have a reason for a search warrant."

"You do."

"What? My girlfriend thinks he looks guilty?" He shook his head.

"I'm telling you, he knows something."

"Claudia!"

"What?"

"Stop it. You're going to get me fired. Yelling out threats at people's doors. Forcing your foot into their homes. You can't do things like that."

"I'm sorry, now let's go to the store and check out his story. I say he's lying."

They waited fifteen minutes for Mrs. Robbin to arrive at the store. She never showed. "Let's go back and make him talk. Scare him a bit."

"I can't do that. It's illegal. You know that."

"I didn't say it wasn't."

"Claudia, stop it."

"I'm telling you he knows something. Look at the woods. They're soaking wet from last night. No one is going to take a short cut through them."

Jessie tapped his fingers on the steering wheel. "All right, Claudia. I'll drive back to his house, but you stay in the car."

"I'll stay in the car. His carpet and floors should be dry by now. You should be able to go inside."

He ignored her. It was enough for him that she promised to stay in the car. He went up to the door and knocked.

As soon as he engaged in conversation with Brian Robbin, Claudia left the car and walked out behind the house. She didn't trust Brian. It was his eyes, his mouth, his everything. Maybe, it was the way he stood, how his voice sounded, or the words he chose to use. She did not know what had given him away, but she knew that she didn't trust him.

Jessie was sitting in the car waiting. He was angry when she returned to the car. "Where did you go?"

She got into the car. "Just a walk."

"Where?"

"On the back of his property."

"Claudia, that's trespassing."

"No, it's police work."

"I don't have a warrant to do that."

"Well, you didn't do it so don't worry about it."

"What I should do is arrest you for trespassing."

"What did he say?"

"He said that she must have went somewhere else."

"He's guilty."

"I can't arrest him, Claudia, just because you think that he looks guilty."

"Jessie, stop telling me what you can't do and start telling me what you can do."

"I can be certain that you'll never be selected for jury duty."

"Jessie, I'm telling you that I'm right about this. It's not a hunch."

"And, Claudia, I'm telling you that there is nothing I can do without some proof."

"He's hiding his wife from us."

Jessie looked at Claudia. He knew that he would never sway her to give up this idea about Brian Robbin knowing something about Nancy's whereabouts. He promised that he would stakeout the house to appease her.

As the night wore on, Jessie and Claudia never saw Mrs. Robbin come home. "This is odd. She cleans the place and leaves. When you were up at the door, Jessie, could you smell any cleaning products?"

"I didn't pay attention." He scooted closer to her and wrapped his right arm around her pulling her towards him. He leaned over and tried to kiss her.

Claudia elbowed him in the ribs. "What the hell's the matter with you? My best friend is missing."

"I'm sorry." He rubbed his ribs where she'd hit him. "Claudia, that hurt."

"How could you be so damn insensitive?"

"Insensitive? I'm going out of my way here. First of all, I'm off duty. This isn't even my assignment. I could get into loads of trouble if the department found out that I was letting you ride around in the car that I technically borrowed from the station. And, furthermore, she is not even legally missing yet. Adults are not legally missing until after…."

Claudia elbowed him again in the same spot. "Don't lecture me about the police department's stupid rules."

"They are the state rules."

"I don't care. They're stupid and so are you. How could you go up to his door and not even try to see or smell anything?"

"Calm down."

"What if he's hurting her, killing her, while we're sitting out here like a bunch of dummies?"

"Claudia, what you don't seem to understand is that we do not have the right to suspect someone of a crime without some sort of evidence."

"Oh, so we have to sit here and wait for her to come crawling half alive out of his house first?"

"That's it. We're leaving."

"Don't take me home. Just let me out."

"No."

Claudia yelled at him until he finally let her out. When he did, she was in front of Ken Barton's store. She was slightly upset that he had never looked back as he drove away from her.

From the store, she phoned Ellen Portson. Knowing her delicate condition, she was careful choosing her words. Soon, it was done. She was invited to stay the night at the Portsons' house. Mr. Barton offered to drive her over there. He said that he was headed over there anyway. He wanted to talk to his wife before going home.

It grew pitch dark out. Sleeping was no option, not while Nancy was missing. Claudia borrowed a flashlight from Mrs. Portson. Without any contemplation, she slipped out of the house and hiked over to the Robbins' place. She told herself that she didn't need Jessie or anyone for that matter.

The backyard looked eerie at night. In the day, it had looked friendly, but now with the dark woods surrounding it, shivers ran up and down her spine just to look at it. Again, she reminded herself that she could do this alone. Her stakeout would take place behind the little playhouse. Here, she would sit and watch for any suspicious action by Brian. Not even ten minutes went by, before she saw him exit the house from the back door. He made a beeline for the shed. Three large dogs were following him. Claudia cursed under her breath. Oddly, they did not detect her. They had a preoccupation with barking at the shed. Even after Brian reentered the house five minutes later, they continued growling, barking, and howling at the shed. Brian called them into the house, but they wouldn't obey him. He had to go out and chase them into the house.

Claudia knew her destination now. Quietly, she made her way over to the shed. The door was locked. She went around the back of it and used her flashlight to size up the window. It would be a tight fit, but she thought she could make it. After locating a big stone, she went to hit the window with it, but stopped her hand just before contact was made. What was she thinking? She wondered if she had a brain at all. How could she break the window without making any sound? Burglary stories ran through her memory. Tape, she'd need some tape. Time was precious, but if she got caught breaking into Brian's shed, she might be looking at time in a different way, in some form of a sentence. Claudia contemplated no further. She ran all the way back to the Portsons' house.

Breathing hard, she tried to quietly enter the house. Once inside, she turned on the kitchen light and hunted wildly for some tape. Ellen awoke and was soon standing behind Claudia. One turn from Claudia and her elbow touched Ellen's hand. Claudia heard herself screaming. Ellen screamed too. Mrs. Barton awoke and phoned Sheriff Clifford.

Poor Ellen, Claudia thought. Luckily, she had not given her a heart attack. "I'm sorry. I didn't mean to scare you. I was looking for some tape."

"This drawer, dear." Ellen moved slowly over to a drawer by the far cabinets. Her hands were still shaking when she handed Claudia the large roll of masking tape.

"What is going on?" Frieda Barton stood at the entrance of the kitchen.

"Oh, Frieda, it's nothing. Claudia just wanted some tape," Ellen explained.

"At this time of night?"

"Well, I can't explain why. It would take too long." Claudia wished they would both go back to sleep. "I'll be right back. I have to go do something."

She took off out the door and ran through the backyard. They watched her in puzzlement. "What's she going to do?" Frieda asked.

Ellen shook her head. "I don't know. I guess she needs to tape something."

Claudia wasted no more time. She quickly placed strip after strip of tape across the window until it was covered. With a big rock in hand, she broke the glass. Then, she peeled the tape away with the broken glass stuck to it. Getting herself hoisted up and in through the open space was now the problem. She heaved, jumped, and cursed herself for not having exercised in months. Finally, she pulled herself in and then maneuvered herself onto the window. Steadying herself with her one hand against the wall and shining the flashlight with her other hand, she saw that the floor was clear for landing and jumped down.

Cautiously, she moved through the shed. "Nancy," she whispered. "Nancy." As she went to take another step near some gardening tools, she heard a thump sound. "Nancy, is that you?" Another thump sounded. Claudia followed the sound. It was near her feet somewhere. She shined the light towards a large cardboard box to her right. The thump came again. The side of the box moved. Slowly, she opened the top. Out jumped a hissing cat. Claudia screamed. A cat, all this for a cat. It was all she could think as she pictured herself before the judge trying to explain her intentions for breaking and entering a shed on someone's property. She'd been wrong and now was busy making a mad rush towards the window.

Quickly, she crawled out, not even remembering how she had managed it. Running to the Portsons' house, she saw a police car approaching the driveway. Its siren was screeching and the red and blue lights were colorfully circling the area. Entering through the back door, she hoped that she had not been noticed. Sheriff Clifford was just entering through the front door as Claudia was entering the living room from the kitchen. She'd made it.

It had boiled down to the fact that he was called by Mrs. Barton when she had heard Claudia and Ellen scream. They all laughed about how Mrs. Barton had forgotten to call the sheriff and tell him not to come after all. Then, what Claudia knew was coming, came. Frieda Barton wanted to know why she needed the tape and where she had gone with it. Claudia skirted around the question with, "it's a long story, and I'm tired. Perhaps I could tell you tomorrow."

Sheriff Clifford watched Claudia yawn several times and soon picked up on the hint. After he left, Ellen and Frieda returned to their rooms. Claudia went to hers but quickly returned to the living room. She then went out and sat on the porch swing wondering if she'd be arrested tomorrow when the Robbins showed the police their shattered window glass, that was neatly stuck to a huge patch of tape.

CHAPTER 23

▼

THE TAPE

The boy cried out loudly. "Daddy. Daddy, help me!"

Brian had been sitting in the living room in the dark when he heard his son's urgent plea. He jumped up from his chair and ran into his son's bedroom. Switching the light on, he saw that Brian Junior's eyes were large with terror and wet with tears. He lifted him out of his bed and gave him a hug. The boy's skin was hot and even his green baseball pajamas were warm. There was sweat across his forehead.

He carried his son into the living room and turned on a lamp. Brian sat in a chair and placed the boy on his lap. Hugging him, he said softly, "Everything will be okay."

"Daddy, it was a monster chasing me. It looked just like Godzilla."

"Like Godzilla! Did he do this to you? Rrrroar!" He tickled his son.

"Daddy, stop," Brian Junior laughed.

"Roarrr!" He tickled him some more.

"Daddy, stop." He laughed.

Brian stopped. "Are you ready to go back to bed?"

"Daddy, when is Mommy coming home? When?"

"Let's go find her and bring her home. Do you want to do that?"

"Yes," he answered excitedly.

"Go change out of those pajamas."

When Brian pulled away from the house, Jessie followed behind him. He'd been waiting for Brian to make his move. He had watched Claudia go back and forth from the Portsons' place to the Robbins' backyard. He had followed her on foot and watched her break into the shed. When she screamed, he almost broke in after her, but she came out so fast that he did not have time to go in. He watched her run back over to the Portsons' house. He looked into the shed with his flashlight and spotted the cat.

Brian sped up, and Jessie stayed back by traveling slowly with his lights off. He radioed Sheriff Clifford. "He's on the move traveling east from his home, over."

"Ten-four." Sheriff Clifford was parked behind Ken Barton's store. He watched Brian's car turn the corner. "I'm on his tale now, over."

"Ten-four." Jessie saw Claudia sitting out on the Portsons' porch swing. She was just a shadow, but he knew her silhouette anywhere. He pulled quickly into the driveway and waited for her to get into his car.

"He just drove down the road," she said.

"I know. We're following him." He gave her a quick kiss on the lips and continued his route down the road. "Claudia, what were you doing in his shed?"

"You saw me?"

"What were you doing? You could have blown everything."

"I thought she was in the…"

Sheriff Clifford's voice rang out from Jessie's car speaker. "He's pulled into the parking lot of the movie house, over."

Jessie picked up his mike. "Right behind you, ten-four."

He glanced at Claudia. "I told Sheriff Clifford what you thought about Brian, so he questioned him, and his story about his wife not being at home was different than what he told us. He told the sheriff that she was visiting her aunt."

After Brian and his son went into the movie house, the sheriff and Jessie pulled their cars into the parking lot. Sheriff Clifford was already up at the movie house entrance. Jessie turned to Claudia. "Stay in the car."

"But why? What if Nancy's in there?"

"Claudia, stay in the car. I mean it."

"Oh, all right."

As soon as Jessie entered the building, Claudia exited the car and followed him into the movie house. She went down the dark hall and up to the little makeshift theater, the large room with cushioned chairs and a big screen. The only light in the room was coming from the large blue glowing TV screen.

Brian Junior ran up to his mother who was lying in a chair with her legs resting on another one. "Mommy, there you are. Daddy and I came to get you."

Brian slowly walked up behind his family. Ireen was now wide-awake. She stood up and hugged her son.

Claudia stayed back by the entrance to the room. Jessie frowned at her. She shrugged her shoulders. Sheriff Clifford scooted over a bit, making room for Claudia.

Ireen hugged her husband. He started crying and hugged her back. Brian Junior looked surprised. "Daddy, you're crying. Daddies don't cry."

Nancy was in the farthest corner of the room sleeping across two chairs. She awoke to Brian Junior's voice. Her neck, back, and legs were stiff, and her head ached from watching tape after tape in the fast forward mode. She looked over at Brian and Ireen hugging each other, and she knew that Ireen had forgiven him.

It dawned on her that it was very late and that she had been here since early this morning when Brian had dropped her and Ireen off. It wasn't easy, but she had convinced him that she would help him. He brought her into his house last night, and he woke his wife. He had Nancy tell his wife his story because he could not. Ireen was certain that she remembered taking the tape off the top of the refrigerator, and because of the title, she put it into the collection of violent shows in the PAVS archives over at the movie house where the group met every third Monday. Even though it had been over a year, Ireen swore she remembered the tape because she had found it in such an odd place. Now, after having scanned nearly two hundred tapes, it was on Nancy's lap.

The bright lights came on overhead, and they turned to see the sheriff, the policeman, and Claudia. Nancy stood up, and her friend rushed over and gave her a big hug. "I was so worried."

"I'm sorry, Claudia. I've been searching for this tape." She held it up. "I had to find it. I promised Brian that I'd help him."

"Don't you think that you could have called somebody? Told them where you were or at least that you were safe?"

"I promised that I wouldn't talk to anyone until I found the tape."

"What is on the tape?" Sheriff Clifford asked.

Ireen went home, taking Brian Junior with her. Nancy put the tape labeled cartoons into the VCR. While it had been a very tense experience watching it with Ireen, it was just as tense watching it again with Brian, Sheriff Clifford, Officer Jessie Richards and Claudia.

They watched Brian torment Jane with his camera, and they witnessed her threaten him with the knife. Everyone gasped when Jane fell on the blade. They heard Brian saying that he wanted to help her. Jane was screaming for him not to touch her. The last they saw of Jane, she was running from the barn. A very slight second of a shot showed Dr. Kebler approaching the driveway. The puzzle was complete at last.

CHAPTER 24

▼

FREEDOM

When Philip came home, the town threw him a party. The Ports-ons' place was alive with music and conversation. Ed and Ellen stuck next to Philip's side most of the day, overjoyed that their boy was home. Brian Junior gave Philip his dog.

Philip hugged his dog. "I'm going to name you Happy."

Claudia walked up to Nancy and handed her a copy of *The Doverlain Daily*. She had circled the article by Sally.

Nancy smiled. "Well, it's about time."

"She did a good job too."

Nancy focused on Chief Randall's, Dr. Kebler's, Gary Saster's, and Richard Fellow's pictures in the newspaper. "Looks like they'll be having their own trials to worry about."

"They deserve to be punished." Claudia looked over by the driveway and saw Jessie's car. "My guy's here. I've got to go."

Claudia hugged Nancy and left with her boyfriend. As they drove down the road, they saw Brian Robbin pushing a sign into the ground that read, House For Sale. Claudia had seen his wife and child at the party. She knew why Brian wasn't there. He wasn't wel-come. The town's people had ousted him. No one would say as little as hello to him, not after what he had done to Jane and Philip. Accident or not, he was the cause of her picking up that knife. His cowardly behavior not to bring the tape forward caused Philip to suffer over a year in prison. While Brian Robbin was found not guilty by the court's legal system, the public's opinion system was much more critical of judging his moral behavior.

Nancy enjoyed the party. She stepped back and observed the people enjoying themselves and celebrating Philip's return. The atmosphere was relaxing and at the same time exciting. She felt a soft hand lightly touch her back.

Mrs. Portson smiled at her. "You did it, Nancy. You brought Philip home. I don't know how Ed and I will ever thank you."

Nancy smiled back. "Ellen, you already have."

These small town people had proven to Nancy that acceptance and love combined created a great power that could work miracles. Philip had come to them as a homeless stranger, and they had taken him in and made him family. Their love had transformed a mentally challenged young man into the gifted artist that he was. Their generosity gave him a place to grow, people to love, and a chance to express himself. Now that he was back home, everyday his medical prognosis was rapidly improving. Philip was becoming stronger and healthier, and his tumor was shrinking.

CHAPTER 25

▼

VACATION

It was a beautiful day. The sun was shining through the window making Nancy's whole apartment bright and lively. She looked at her large painting on the wall of the colorful woods in Denten and the cool blue lake where the young man, Philip, stood fishing with his dog beside him. This was Philip's present to her for all of her help. He called the picture, "The Free Man."

Nancy heard a knock at the door. It was Claudia. The first words out of her mouth were, "you can't take a vacation now."

"The boss said that I could have three weeks off."

"That's way too long. You don't realize how much work I'll have to do while you're gone. I'll have to check every story that goes into the paper. That replacement for you doesn't know how to scrutinize anything. He'll let everything slide through, and I'll have to try and catch every mistake before it goes to print."

"I'm really proud of you for putting Sally on all of those assignments."

"Prove it. Cut your vacation down to one week."

"I can't. I'm going on a Caribbean cruise for three weeks, and my parents already paid for the ticket."

"Must be nice to have Mommy and Daddy paying for everything?"

"It is, and don't try to make me feel like a spoiled child because it won't work."

"I'll tell you what, Nancy. You can do a piece about the cruise for the travel section."

"No, I'll be on vacation, besides, I'm an editor. We wouldn't want to break any contract agreements especially since we fought for them during the strike."

Claudia rolled her eyes. "Fine, you have fun on your vacation," she told her as she was leaving.

"Do you mean it?"

"No."

"Admit it, Claudia, you are green with envy." Nancy yelled down the hall after her.

Nancy easily forgot those thoughtless words to her friend. The first week of her vacation was spent not thinking about anyone except herself and how much fun and relaxation that she was enjoying. Two more weeks of this and she'd think that she was in Heaven.

Most of the people were single and around her age. That was her mother's doing, who had made sure that her daughter would be on the singles cruise ship. There were some definite prospects here: The gentleman who she had danced with the first night, the one she had eaten dinner with the second night, and the one she had gone swimming with everyday. Already, one man had proposed to her. If he had not been such a joker, she might have taken him seriously. Last night, she had stayed with a group of people who were watching the stars and discussing astronomy. This was a highly intellectual conversation led by two astronomy professors. This cruise was a smorgasbord of interesting and fun people where anything could happen. If her mother were lucky, what she had hoped for would happen.

Nancy could not believe all of the fun that she was having. Her first week had been like a dream come true: all play and no work. This was just one of those moments in her life when everything was going perfect, and she wanted to cherish every second of it. Two more weeks left and her body was still tingling with excitement. Every morning was like the first day of spring.

Deep into her own thoughts of relaxation with her eyes closed, she was enjoying the gentle warm wind brush over her entire body, massaging it as she listened to soothing music and a few voices sharing quiet conversations. The gentle motion of the ship and the wind were rocking Nancy asleep in paradise.

"You are as pretty as a picture."

Nancy's eyes flew open. Widely, they stared in disbelief. "Jimmy! What are you doing here?" she shouted.

"Is that anyway to greet a friend? Aren't you excited to see me?"

"What are you doing here?"

He pulled a lounge chair over by her and plopped his pale white body into it. She was definitely seeing more of him than she wanted to. The bright orange swim trunks were practically blinding her.

Jimmy smiled at her with that flirting smile of his that for some reason always irritated her. "You will never believe this, Nancy, but I'm here on an assignment. *The Doverlain Daily* wouldn't give me my old job back. The union backed me, and so the head honcho as Claudia calls him offered me the travel section. It's not what I'm used to, but when Claudia told me that you would be my editor, I said yes. Then, Claudia pushed the honcho to put me on this cruise. I boarded last night." He looked out at the ocean and the sky. "It's just grand isn't it?"

Nancy was speechless. This was like hearing someone say that the Titanic was unsinkable, and then it sank. Her mind raced with questions. What did I say? What did I do? How did this happen?

Jimmy smiled big. "Claudia said to tell you that you were right; she's green with envy. Oh, and she hopes your last two weeks are memorable. Isn't she a sport?"

The End!

About the Author

Kelly Phillips holds a master's degree in education, a bachelor's degree in English, and a minor in psychology from the University of Michigan. Phillips has raised two sons. She lives in Romulus, Michigan with her husband.

978-0-595-37254-
0-595-37254-6